NARROW ROOMS

Other Books by James Purdy

Color of Darkness
Malcolm
The Nephew
Children is All
Cabot Wright Begins
Eustace Chisholm and the Works
Jeremy's Version
I Am Elijah Thrush
The Running Sun (Poetry)
The House of the Solitary Maggot
In a Shallow Grave
A Day after the Fair (Stories and Plays)

NARROW ROOMS

JAMES PURDY

14

ARBOR HOUSE
New York

For
James Michael Tillotson
and
Stephen D. Adams

THE HUMAN EMBRYO is curled up in a ball with the nostrils placed between the two knees.

At death the pupil opens wide.

Vance De Lakes waited an interminable while in Dr. Ulric's office. Every few seconds he would lose courage and make a motion to leave. The smell of carbolic acid, chloroform, whatever it was, always made Vance a little light-headed in any case, and looking through the two medical books whose quoted sentences are above was as nauseating as the smells. There were extremely few magazines in the waiting room, and most of these were of interest only to farmers. *The National Geographic* was the only reading matter Vance could stand to open but "The South Seas Today," and "The New Eskimo,"

1

and the disappearance of the puffin, to tell the truth, did not mean too much to him.

"It's about Sidney." Vance had begun volubly when the Doctor stood before him gazing under knitted brows, and extending his hand which Vance did not take only because he did not see it.

Following the Doctor into his study, Vance shot a hasty look into the room on the left and saw a still fairly young man (who looked like somebody he had seen working on the highway) stretched out on a couch, his hands lavishly bandaged.

"I won't take but a minute of your time, Doc," Vance began. He held a big straw hat in his hands which he wore to protect his head from the boiling August sun, but in his haste to get to the doctor's he had forgotten to put it on, and had carried it as one would a parcel.

The particular news which he had borne, the medicinal hospital smells, the brief glimpse of the man with the blood-stained bandages had made Vance begin to keel over, but the doctor quickly pushed his head down, and then seeing he was not going to pass out, pressed a smelling bottle to his nose.

"It's Sidney, Doc," Vance had begun, lifting his head up, and gazing helplessly at the physician. "He's come home. . . . But don't start so, Doc . . . It's all right . . . He's been pardoned. He's a free man."

That was how it began. Sidney was sent home from prison to us, pardoned, but he hadn't been able to pardon what he felt about himself.

Sidney was a big fellow when he was sent up, and his extreme size made him look older than he was. At fifteen people sometimes took him for draft age.

Now when he came home from prison he looked considerably smaller, and younger. He looked almost as young as his kid brother Vance, who was twenty.

There were times now after he had got back when Sidney would go into his brother's bedroom and behave as if he was going to ask Vance something, his mouth would open slightly and all the time he tried to speak he looked like he had been slapped. He really looked slapped all the time. Then having said nothing he would stare in the direction of Vance as if he was the author of all his pain.

"It hurts me more than anything else ever did," Vance was explaining to Dr. Ulric now. "Sidney don't want to go out to see anybody, and he's not happy either when he's with me. . . ."

"Why force him then?" the Doc retorted, smoking one of those dilapidated-looking black cigarettes he had been puffing on for forty years. "Don't do anything, Vance, at this time . . . That's often the best way to deal with a problem. Most problems. Sort of let it go away from you . . . You mind me now, do you hear? . . . But I would like him to come to see me . . . Anytime at all tell him. But don't you do anything right now. There's nothing you can do anyhow but let him know he's still your brother. . . ."

"But it was me who visited him in the pen," Vance spoke like one defending himself. "Who else went there week after week, far as it is from here . . . And he never appreciated it! . . . All he ever asked about was Gareth Vaisey." (Gareth was a neighbor boy who had been in a serious auto wreck about the time of Sidney's trouble.)

"But, Vance, see it's you he has come home to! . . . He didn't come home to Gareth after all. . . ."

Vance quieted down. Dr. Ulric had that ability to calm one,

not so much by what he said, he said very little, but by reason of his being himself so quiet. Then he had delivered most of the babies for twenty-five miles around and perhaps the two speakers remembered at this moment ever so fleetingly that the doctor had delivered both Sidney and Vance. He was after all considerably closer to many of his patients than a father. *Too close,* the doctor often thought. Hence perhaps his insomnia.

"I'm too close to everybody," Dr. Ulric had once said in a loud voice when he had had a glass too many of the huckleberry wine which he manufactured himself down in the basement.

As he neared seventy Dr. Ulric's face began to set in a certain way so that it resembled a door that has been nailed shut in a deserted house. His eyes were as bright as ever, perhaps brighter, the disc of the pupil appearing to move like a white fire, but his face in general gave the impression of belonging to someone who never expected anything again. His present was taken up with tasks which he held onto like a drowning man will to the sight of shore. Yes, his patients were as needful to him as air, and his ministrations were therefore not duty but necessity. And though his hands trembled too badly for him to deliver babies (it was his skill as an obstetrician which had given him his greatest reputation), he toiled from early to late with the sick and the discouraged.

He had leased out the many acres of fields surrounding his house to farmers to grow corn on. There was something about the sight of the corn—in the summer growing taller and heavier and then the gold sheaves in the fall and winter— which were nearly as important to him as his patients.

Sometimes in mid-August he would walk out at some considerable distance into the cornfields and appear to be listening to the moving stalks.

The night Sidney De Lakes had shot Brian McFee to death at the Bent Ridge Tavern, Doc had paid no particular attention to the dead youth lying on the sawdust of the floor. It was the one charged with the shooting he turned his attention to; Sidney towered up all his six feet three inches, chest out, his back pressed tight against the wall, his palms slightly upraised, a cold sweat pouring down over his forehead and upper lip so that he appeared to be standing under a leaking eavespipe.

The Doc had opened his bag, called for a tumbler of water from the white-lipped bartender, and taking up a tiny envelope containing powder, dropped some into the glass, stirred and then forced the solution past the clenched teeth of the new-fledged murderer whose head had immediately fallen over the doctor's hand as if to kiss or perhaps bite it. Doc had never seen Sidney since that day four years ago.

Brian McFee, aged twenty, had raised his gun at Sidney and threatened to fire because of an alleged insult during some heated argument which had arisen while they had been hunting together that day, prior to their going to the Bent Ridge Tavern. Sid, who was of course armed also, had (his lawyer later claimed) fired involuntarily, at least in self-defense, when he saw Brian was raising his gun at him again, and the bullet from that shot had hit Brian in the left eye, killing him instantly.

During the trial in response to a question from the prosecution as to whether he was "sorry" or not for what he had done, Sidney at first had replied *"I am not sorry,"* which his own lawyer later had attempted to explain away owing to his "rattled" mental condition, but again under cross-examination, Sidney had blurted out with regard to Brian: "He had hounded me for months, worried and nagged me each day . . . I am not sorry that nagging and worrying is over . . . But I cared . . . deeply for Brian McFee." (He had added this statement also against the wishes or advice of his defender.)

To make his case worse, Sidney refused to tell the court or even his own attorney what was the nature of Brian's harassment and nagging of him, and the exact origin of his quarrel with the dead boy. Sidney refused to speak at greater length about the shooting thereafter, and no one else could come forward to offer an explanation, not even his brother Vance, to whom the whole affair remained a gloomy puzzle.

Sidney was sent up for manslaughter.

Dr. Ulric had received a letter from Sidney about two months after he had started to serve his sentence. It contained only one line, with no salutation or leave-taking. It read:

> See that Vance makes something of himself.
> (Signed) Sidney De Lakes.

Vance had thought the sun rose and set in Sidney, or so everybody said, but you didn't need anybody to say it for you, you just had to watch. Dr. Ulric had once seen Vance lacing up Sidney's boots at the start of hunting season. There was a peaceful expression on the boy's face which recalled the look some people have when receiving the host. It had given the doctor pause.

The day or rather the morning after Sidney had killed his hunting companion, Vance had been afraid to go home. With his brother already in jail, he had been ashamed to be seen on the streets. For a while he had thought he would step into the First Presbyterian Church and occupy one of the back pews, but even here he was sure he would be observed or that his presence in the church be explained as counterfeit piety. Later

6

on for a while he had gone into the depths of the cornfield behind Doc Ulric's. Both the moving corn and the lights from the doctor's house comforted him. But the damp in the cornfield (it was rather cold for August) and a rat running over his shoes made him, together with the terror of returning to an empty house, go up the back steps of the doctor's house and rap on the screen door.

"I wondered when you'd show up," Dr. Ulric had said. "Sit over there why don't you . . ."

Another peculiar thing about Dr. Ulric was that though known for his bountifulness, compassion and devotion to the lives of his patients he was almost never seen to smile. His face was not sour or bitter, nonetheless, but some said (perhaps wrongly) that it was disappointed in aspect.

Vance had kept the tears back with the firmness and strength of a man who is determined to hang himself albeit with a poor cord, but now seated in the best chair in the house, with the doctor smoking peaceably nearby, and with the quiet of the countryside broken only by the songs of crickets and katydids, short convulsive sobs rose out of the corner he occupied.

Dr. Ulric's one pleasure in life outside of his dark imported cigarettes was, when he got started, talking—talking not so much to you as around you, it didn't matter who the patient was when he got started. He had been known also to talk to his cat, and these lengthy speeches usually touched on medicine, and came helped by his having read most of the 5,000 books in his library which spilled all over his fifteen-room pillared house.

Vance had always been grateful that the doctor had talked that night not about the shooting and his brother but about bread, and that he had made no comment on his weeping until when it had got somewhat beyond control Doc stepped into the next room, fetching out some sort of surgical dressing "for you to bawl on, Vance."

The Doctor had then continued his speech about (and Vance listened while choking back his sobs) the uses of bread in medical dressings from earliest recorded history up to today. Bread was once applied in water and oil or rosewater to soften abscesses (Vance would nod after a sentence or two of these bits of information). Mixed in wine it was for centuries used to treat bruises and sprains; stale bread or sailor's bread, pounded and then baked again, was a remedy for looseness of the bowels. In wine again it was applied to swollen eyes (a quick glance toward and then away from the inconsolable one). Persons suffering from palsy were given bread soaked in water, immediately after bathing or fasting . . . With strong vinegar, stale bread was used to dissolve calluses on the feet. . . .

"Let me stay on with you, Doc!" Vance had burst forth at last. "I can't go back to that house alone, can I?"

And without waiting for a response to this plea, Sidney's brother sang out: "Do you think they will send him to the electric chair?"

"I do *not,*" the doctor replied immediately.

"Oh, thank you, thank you for saying that," Vance murmured.

The first week he was back Sidney did not go out of the house at all. The beginning of the second week, around midnight, he came out of his sleeping room barefoot and walked through the parlor where Vance was mending a jacket belonging to his brother (he came out of jail with hardly a stitch to put on, and most of his old clothes didn't look right on him anymore). Neither of the brothers exchanged a word. Vance could follow him with his eye as Sid strolled outdoors and passed into the little apple orchard, and finally sauntering over to a weathered bench he elected to sit down. After a long while he picked up a green eating apple resting at his feet, but did not offer to taste it, holding it gloomily and loosely in his hand.

Vance stopped sewing on his brother's jacket; he averted his face slightly so that he would not seem to be staring at Sidney. Then he put out the lamp, leaving only the hall light burning. He walked over to the fireplace and poked the moribund ashes.

Almost before he knew it, Vance too had gone out to the apple orchard and seated himself next to Sidney on the bench.

"You got to go out by daytime too, Sid," he commenced.

"Who says so?" came the crabby rejoinder.

"You got to face them eventually . . ."

"Why can't we move from here?" Sidney wondered, touching Vance's shoulder ever so lightly with his outstretched fingers. "Light out . . ."

"And leave the house and everything . . . ?"

"Sell it."

"Who'd buy it, Sid . . . It's most finished . . . See how dilapidated it looks even by starlight . . . It's all but turned to powder."

Vance waited in silence a while. Sid took his hand then in his, pressed it, then let it go.

"We could go swimming tomorrow over at Barstow's . . . Sid, you always was a good swimmer and diver."

"Yeah, I guess you thought so . . . anyhow. . . ."

The next day they set off about ten o'clock for Barstow's. They walked through the south end of the cornfield which eventually showed up on Doc Ulric's property, then past a stretch of cottonwood trees, up quite a sandy bluff, and at last down to the river itself.

Vance had stripped and had secured his clothes partly under some stones and was already in the water. Sidney, gazing at the river from the edge of the shore, dispiritedly undressed, but then at the last moment, although having already wet his feet to go in, he stood stock still, lifting his nose like a deer that smells danger.

A young man, about Sidney's age, had just crossed down the sloping path that led to the river in his truck, behind which was a trailer with two young horses inside who were whinnying and kicking vehemently, one of them making the attempt despite the cramped quarters and narrow confinement to rear on his hind legs. The truck driver came to a halt, and staring at Sidney thunderstruck, had jumped out of his vehicle and advanced a few steps still wearing the awestruck look on his countenance.

Both Vance and Sidney recognized him as the "son of the renderer," also called by the villagers the "scissors-grinder," and between whom and the De Lakes brothers there had always been "bad blood," almost a kind of obscure and muted feud which many claimed was behind Brian McFee's having been shot to death.

Roy Sturtevant, the newcomer or "renderer," had stopped then, his bewilderment, if anything, increasing, and he had stretched out his hands finally not to greet Sidney or embrace him but as a further, and involuntary, expression of his incredulity and amazement at seeing De Lakes.

Sidney flinched and drew back several paces, for, as he was

later to explain to Vance, the very sight of a man's hands coming toward him since he had been in prison made him uneasy, but to see Roy Sturtevant approaching him in this fashion, unexpected as his coming had been also, was more than he could bear. It brought back to him in a dizzying rush all the terrible events which had led up to his having been convicted and imprisoned.

The "renderer" (actually only his Grandfather had ever really been in such a distasteful occupation, but both his son and Roy Sturtevant went on being called thus) slowly dropped his hands at his sides, blinked his eyes, and got out: "So, it's you after all!" and then having spoken this, perhaps only to himself, he rushed back to his truck and trailer and disappeared, rousing his horses by his violent hurry to whinny and kick and even threaten to bite one another.

Vance slowly, almost mournfully, turned away from this brief spectacle of the meeting between two men who had long had some unspoken conflict between them which he had never begun to understand or wanted to understand, and he strove to swim out toward the direction of the little hills which he was always able to see from Dr. Ulric's spacious back windows. When finally he turned round facing shore, he saw Sidney still listlessly stationed at the river's edge, brooding and oblivious to anything around him.

"What did he want?" Vance wondered, toweling his dripping body, and it was then he saw the marks on Sid. He quickly turned away from looking at them so as not to embarrass him any more than he was already embarrassed. The marks or scars looked like somebody had decorated him with razor thrusts about his chest, and on past to his back and up and down his spine; red wales such as come from scourging were visible.

"Search me, Vance," Sidney replied, a strange look both sad

and almost ecstatic on his face. He began splashing the brown river water over his breast as if to draw attention now to the scars themselves, but then he held his hands and arms over the long row of irregularly healed wounds and blinked before he dove into the water. Vance watched him swim until his head was only a shiny black dot on the river.

Sidney refused to go swimming again after that day, and Vance did not urge it again.

"I do hate to leave you all alone by yourself," Vance would say as their day's routine began in earnest now, "but as I wrote you, I work for the doctor in his office nowadays . . . Sort of an all-round helper. I type up his prescriptions, chauffeur for him, and prepare some of his meals, and keep his out-of-town appointments straightened out."

Sidney nodded, but Vance was not certain his brother had even heard him.

"This evening I thought we'd take a little stroll uptown after it cools off," Vance finished with forced pleasantness.

Sidney did not nod this time and appeared even further absorbed in his own musing, but just before Vance went out for the day the older boy smiled faintly and that cheered his brother so considerably that he went down the steps whistling.

"We strolled down Main street," Vance confided later to the doctor . . . "Sid tightened up the minute we began passing the shopwindows and he saw his reflection in the glass . . . . I realized after a bit he didn't at first recognize the reflection the windows was his own, he had changed so in every which way while he was in jail that he thought at first he was looking at the face of a stranger. He kept staring at himself in the glass. . . . We walked on then and pretty soon passed the Royal movie house which he had attended as a boy. Then we began to meet people we both half-knew or knew casually, and they nodded and sort of grinned, sickly-like, and that made things worse. . . . He walked like a man does through a gauntlet, with his mouth set and his jaw tight, and dim eyes. . . . Then we went into the Sweet Shop and seated ourselves clear in the back out of notice. . . . Oh, why did we do it after all? . . . We ordered sodas . . . well, he couldn't drink his, and I wasn't able to finish mine. . . . But anyhow he did it! He *appeared*! But on the way back he turned to me and said, *'Don't ever ask me to go to town again, hear?'* And then in rapid fire he says, 'Did you see who was sittin' in the seat directly facing ours? . . . No? Well, it was *him* . . .' "

"Him?" Vance had replied totally in the dark.

"Yes, *him*, the one who has always been doggin' me ever since I can remember, Vance! You know very well who . . . The renderer!"

"Oh Roy Sturtevant again! Yes, I guess I saw him. But he ain't in that occupation, Sid." Vance heard himself slipping into the bad grammar his brother used and which Vance blamed on jail, forgetting Sid had always used such grammar, had always been a poor "scholar," and that only his glory, short-lived as it had been, as a halfback on the high school football team and a champion swimmer and diver disguised the fact that in all other ways he had never, in the opinion and phraseology of Dr. Ulric's village, "amounted to a hill of beans."

"His Grandfather was the renderer, Sid, a long, long time ago," Vance heard himself repeating this worn bit of information to his brother's deaf ears.

"I never want to set eyes on him again as long as I live . . . I feel he brought me all my bad luck. He was somehow behind my fall!"

Sidney gave his brother a look such as he had never given him before.

Vance gazed in return at him, dumbfounded. And something deep stirred in him, fear, suspicion, dread, perhaps something more and probably worse. He reached for Sid's hand then, but the latter withdrew it. Then aware of the younger fellow's disappointment at his withholding his affection, Sid took his hand tight in his heavy, rough grasp and held it to the point of pain.

"Sidney, why don't you unburden yourself to me? Don't you trust me? I know there probably was something between you and the renderer as you call him, and I have always wondered if maybe your quarrel with him had something to do with the trouble between you and Brian McFee. . . . I mean, Sid . . ."

"Don't, please, don't!" Sidney implored. (He acted, you see, like the younger brother and always had.) "I can't bear no more after what I've went through in prison. But yes, for your information, I guess Roy Sturtevant had a hand in all that happened to me and Brian. . . . Don't ask me to explain it, Vance, for I can't. I mean I don't understand it myself . . . Yes, maybe he's behind it all."

Sidney threw himself now into his brother's arms and held onto him with might and main.

"You know about me anyhow, don't you, Vance?" came his smothered voice. "Don't you?" he cried on, pressing his mouth against his brother's mended jacket. "You're so good, Vance, it's hard to feel worthy of you. You're so straight and upright. . . . I guess maybe you suspicioned about what I am, and must have guessed the truth about Brian and me, that we . . ."

"It don't matter now." Vance broke away from his brother's close embrace. His voice rose to a hysterical wail. "We won't think about any of that . . . It's over and done with. . . ."

"No, Vance, it's not over and done . . . I'm trying to level with you, see, to explain to you. . . . "

"Sid, you're all I've got." Vance spoke now with almost the same fierce incoherence that had been Sidney's a moment before. "It don't matter to me what you've done anyhow . . . I've just waited for you to come back to me. I don't have nothing else to live for. . . ."

"Don't say that, Vance. For God's sake, don't please . . . I'm not worth that much when all's said and done. . . ."

Going up to his brother, Sid spoke almost into the younger boy's teeth: "You've got to find something worthy of you, Vance . . . You're straight, and you ought to marry . . . Don't bank your whole life on somebody like me, hear? . . . Forget me."

"You are my life, Sid."

"I hear . . . ," Sidney began after a long struggle to find his voice. "I hear also you went to the Governor and that you got him to intercede for me."

Vance barely nodded, for his own emotions were so topsy-turvy he dared not risk speaking at that moment.

"I would do it all again," Vance managed finally to tell him, but in a voice so unlike his own Sidney turned quickly and gave him a look of eloquent wonder. "I would lie for you even, Sid, I reckon. Even if you had killed Brian McFee in cold blood . . ."

"Christ, Vance," Sidney turned away. He struggled to keep

down all the feelings that had threatened to erupt ever since his return.

"I know more than you give me credit for, Sid," Vance was going on in this new voice, the voice of a stranger, imbued with and full of his new "knowledge." "I was always pretty sure you thought an awful lot of Brian McFee too."

Sidney nodded many times, and with each nod he pressed Vance's knee with his fingers.

"Since you're getting close, Vance, yes I did . . . I thought an awful lot of him, and he . . . me." Then almost in fury: "Why do you think we went hunting so much anyhow? . . . But in cold blood," he quieted down, "no, I never shot him in cold blood. . . . He felt, you see, I was turning against him . . . I wasn't . . . I was, I mean, trying to gain time to understand my own feelings for him . . . But he couldn't wait. . . . He felt he'd rather die or see me die than lose my caring for him. . . . So he kept shooting at me in the woods that day. . . . I run to the Bent Ridge Tavern . . . But you know it all, Vance . . . Cold blood, never . . ."

"That's all you need to say, Sid. . . . You know I believe you."

"I carry a terrible burden though in my heart, Vance . . . Cold blood, hot blood, whatever you call it . . ."

Sidney buried his face in his hands as he said the last few words. Vance hesitated a long while, then bending over him he pressed his lips to his brother's neck. It was more like he had whispered a secret to him than bestowed a kiss. Sid took Vance's hand again in his, and pressed hard again and again.

"There are these people I suppose who are destined to play parts in our lives," Sidney had said to his brother later that night when Vance had come in to say goodnight to him.

But the thought and the way he pronounced the words

were as unlike the old Sidney as it was possible to be.

"You won't hold it against me now, Vance." The older brother looked up then, perturbed. "For what I've told you tonight, I mean . . ."

Vance shook his head morosely.

"I shouldn't have told you," he whispered in the face of Vance's heavy silence.

"No, no, Sid, you should have," Vance forced a smile. "It's my fault, Sid, for what Mama once explained it as my looking up to you too much. Remember?"

"I guess nobody could look up to me now, Vance, that's for sure."

"That's not so, Sid. I didn't mean that, and you mustn't say it!"

Sid reared up in bed and pushed his back against the bedstead with almost the same kind of wild and frenzied movement as he had the night of the shooting when he had pressed his back against the wall as he stood facing the dying Brian McFee.

"I think more highly of you I believe than ever before," Vance continued doggedly. "I know I am the last person on earth you would want to confide these things to, Sid. That's my fault too. . . . But Sid," and here Vance's own voice took on some of the wildness of his brother's, "promise me one thing, forget this Roy Sturtevant. Nobody can cause another man evil unless the second party involved allows him to . . ."

Sidney stared at his brother like thunderstruck. Then he took him in his arms and kissed him fiercely.

"You don't look on me as stained and dirty then?" Sidney cried in a kind of hopeful buoyancy.

"You know better, Sid."

Vance had not told Sidney he would confide in the doctor, but he had to tell somebody. He had to unburden himself and after all telling the Doc was like whispering it to the river by midnight. Yet he felt somehow he had done wrong. He should have kept Sidney's secret locked in his own heart. He felt suddenly in the first wake of his disappointment and anger that Brian McFee deserved killing.

"So now you know," Vance said with some ill temper in his voice. "Or did you, judging by your expression, did you always know . . . I suppose you did."

"I don't think of people as queer or straight," the Doc said. "Not when you're as old as I. And I don't think God does either."

"I didn't know you believed in God, Doc," Vance said in a choked voice, for his grief was getting the better of him again.

"Well, I believe in the soul I guess, the soul somehow that is *one* and is in everybody. I am not a thinker, Vance."

He kept fingering a piece of paper. Actually it was a letter he had been poring over and debating whether or not to show to Vance.

"You have been worrying about Sidney not having a job," the Doctor began, and Vance did not know whether to shout for joy or to curse the old man for his seeming indifference to his having told of the fall of his idol.

"Isn't that a fact, Vance . . . You wanted for Sidney to have a job."

"It is," Vance replied.

"Look here, my boy," the old man's voice rose. "You have got to brace up now. The worst is over. He's back."

"Is he?" And then he broke down in a way that touched the old man more deeply than when Vance had come to pass the first night he had ever spent without his brother, when Sidney was already in jail and life bore down on him heavily.

"Vance, listen to me. You still have your hero. Do you understand? He *told* you, Vance. He confided. Don't you see he returns your love more than he could return it to another man? Don't you?"

"I want to," he said between his choking and sobbing.

"Now brace up." He went into the adjoining room. He poured something and brought it out.

"I don't want it, Doc. I can take it without that."

"Drink it. It's nothing anyhow. Drink it, and then listen to this letter which comes from Mrs. Vaisey about her son."

He drank and listened.

"You know the Vaisey boy, Gareth?" the Doc began.

"I do of course."

"You remember he was in a train wreck?"

"And he was mixed up with the renderer if my own memory serves me."

The Doctor exchanged a look of real wonder and annoyance with his "charge."

"Gareth was the only one who survived the wreck when the fast train hit the truck and trailer he was driving. His father and Gareth's two brothers died. . . . But later on, whether due to this wreck or his having been thrown from a horse and kicked in the bargain, well, he developed one might say a number of symptoms. He is a virtual invalid and seldom goes out. Gareth is now about twenty . . . His mother needs a caretaker. . . ." He tapped the letter against Vance's cheek.

"No, Doc, no," Vance cried. "Sidney can't do that kind of work."

"Why in thunder can't he?" the Doc exploded. "He can and he must."

"An orderly? A male nurse? Never."

"Then what is he to do?"

Vance's deep silence was the first step toward assent.

When they parted a few minutes later, the Doctor put his arm around Vance and held him to him for a long time. They had never been so close as then, Vance knew, and he had never needed closeness that bad before.

"I learned yesterday of a job that is open, Sid." Vance managed to broach the subject the next morning as he was clearing the breakfast dishes (it was five o'clock in the morning, and outside the fog from the mountains had, if anything, grown more pronounced than at nightfall). "It's thought, I guess, to be a real opportunity for whoever is interested."

"A job I could fill?" Sidney wondered, his feelings still raw from the distance that would always he supposed exist between him and Vance.

"Yes, who else?" Vance's voice took on a real edge. "There's a position vacant at the Vaisey household . . . Taking care of the young man there who was in that unusual train wreck some time back. . . . You remember him, of course."

Sidney blushed beet-red under his prison pallor, and looked down at his toast and eggs.

But Vance himself was so uneasy over bringing up the offer of the "opportunity" for his brother that he did not observe the confusion which the mention of the Vaisey boy's name brought to the job-seeker.

"I thought, matter of fact," Sidney tried to recover his composure, "that maybe Gareth might have . . . died also by now, and that perhaps you had neglected to tell me . . ."

"I guess I should have kept you abreast of his condition," Vance unbent a little, "since you used to inquire about him so often when I came to see you, I recall . . ."

"I guess I hated to keep asking you about him when the subject . . . well, seemed to displease you when I brought it up."

"I'm sorry if I gave you that impression, Sid . . . I should have offered you the news about him more willingly, I reckon. . . . Anyhow, the job there is going begging!" He finished this with a kind of exhausted fury and impatience.

"But, Vance," Sid rose from his breakfast, and with good humor and encouragement in his voice, "you ain't told me what the job is to be . . ."

Turning away from Sid slightly, Vance responded: "The offer comes as a matter of fact from Dr. Ulric, and I was sort of cool to it myself at first . . . But I thought . . ."

"But just tell me what's expected, Vance."

"This . . . Gareth . . . ," Vance tried to control his own reluctance, if not ill humor, "is as you may know a sort of invalid, and needs somebody to take care of him. . . . The other caretakers never stayed more than a few weeks. . . . And Sid, to tell you the truth, I was afraid you might feel it was beneath you. . . ."

Sidney sat down in his chair again, and touched his coffee cup. "Beneath me?" he repeated, seeking for any sarcasm which might lie under this remark; but Vance was incapable, he decided, of sarcasm.

"An invalid now, huh?" Sidney's eyes got that dreamy look they so often had. "In times past all Gareth ever liked to do was ride horses. . . . I remember his Dad told me once that young as he was he was capable of breaking in a horse, and as a matter of fact later I found out he had done so—broke several horses, in fact. . . . His dream was to be in a rodeo, or who knows, a circus . . ."

"But it was by breaking in a horse, I believe, Sid, that he

got injured. At least riding this new horse, which threw him and kicked him also . . . You see Gareth was not injured in the train wreck. Only some little scratches, whilst his Dad and his two younger brothers were killed."

"You know Gareth was part of the gang of boys that clustered round the renderer," Sidney mused.

"Maybe we best drop the idea then, Sid. After all there's plenty of time."

"No, Vance, there ain't, as a matter of fact. There's not much time at all where I'm concerned. I'll take the job if she will give it to me."

"Oh I don't think there's any question she'll offer it to you. She's desperate . . . Excuse me, I didn't mean that the way it sounded. . . ."

"I'll go."

"But, Sid, do you really want to. I can't stand the thought of you emptying chamber pots and paring the toenails of some non-compos-mentis boy . . ."

"But I know Gareth . . ."

This time Vance blushed for he wanted to but did not dare ask more.

"You see, Vance, I can't just sit around here and live off you. . . . I tell you I'll take it." He stood up, and he smiled, and going over to Vance he punched him with his fist in the belly, and smiled broadly.

Mrs. Vaisey had offered to send her chauffeur over to fetch Sidney, but he insisted on walking the six or seven miles.

He was a bit winded by the time he had arrived, nonetheless. His opportunity for exercise in prison had been minimal, and all he had had for keeping in shape were a dilapidated punching bag and some weights. As a result of being confined or (who knows?) because of—as the prison psychiatrist put it—the weight of memory, his heart troubled him to some extent.

Sidney had spruced himself up considerably for the ordeal of meeting Gareth's mother. He had put on one of Vance's Christmas-present dress shirts, a knit tie of neutral color, his dark hair was combed wet, and at the last Vance had insisted on manicuring his nails—Sidney always had had a tendency to keep his nails poorly, with black dirt under them, and the thumb nails more apt than not to be broken. His blue eyes shining in contrast to his extremely dark complexion gave him today a calm handsomeness and purity which was inconsistent with the epithet ex-convict.

Mrs. Vaisey did not keep him waiting long for, contrary to rumor, she was not grand at all; and the story that she was rich merely because she lived in a mammoth mansion was inaccurate. The threat of foreclosure hung over her, and since Gareth's accident, she came to realize that although she had constantly scolded him in years past with his immaturity, when the time came he was no longer himself, she realized then it had been he who had kept at the account books and prevented her from being outright ruined and bankrupt.

Gareth's mother spoke to Sidney without embarrassment or self-consciousness and there was no hint or mention on her part as to where he had been for over four years, and Sidney also felt that perhaps, since she seemed so scatterbrained and forgetful, that she might not really know he had been in prison. So he insisted on telling her at the very beginning of their conference.

"Dr. Ulric has told me all I need know about you," Mrs. Vaisey had affirmed, thus closing any further discussion of this matter.

She was a much younger woman than he had expected,

certainly under forty. Her blonde hair looked untouched by gray, at least in this soft light of the old house; her complexion was a rich creamy color, and the only jarring aspect to her appearance was her hands, which showed the effect of hard work so that one would have thought despite her having hired help she did her own dishes and scrubbed her own floors.

He could tell she was satisfied with him, and she said as much, but though she spoke of Gareth constantly and told of their visits to New York and Chicago to see famous specialists, and complained of the cost, she was, he felt, about to dismiss him for today without having let him look in on his "charge."

"Can I see Gareth now, Mrs. Vaisey?" Sidney finally came to the point.

She looked a bit displeased at this, or rather, hurt. He on the other hand feared that perhaps he was to be hired because of Gareth and yet—who knows?—not be able to set eyes on him.

At last she nodded, and rang a bell. The girl who had admitted him at the front door came in, and Mrs. Vaisey spoke to her in a voice almost too low to be heard by Sidney. "Is Gareth dressed yet? . . . He's had something to eat already? I see. . . . Will you just step in then and tell him I'll be up directly with this young man."

"You won't have something to drink while we're waiting?" she inquired of Sidney. He shook his head.

Sidney somehow had the feeling that they were in a train station, waiting for someone to arrive. But he knew in fact she was stalling for time.

"Life is very hard, Mr. De Lakes . . . But I don't need to tell you." This was her only indication that she had recognized and thought over thoroughly that he had been "in trouble," the phrase people in this village use to cover prison, and being pregnant without a husband.

"I would like more than anything in the world to take the position," he said in a loud voice.

She looked up as surprised as if he had spoken in Greek.

"I was quite prepared to take you before you got here," she replied. "Dr. Ulric has never recommended anyone before."

Just then the young girl appeared again and nodded to her employer. Mrs. Vaisey rose, and asked him to allow her to go on ahead.

He had not been quite prepared for so long a flight of stairs. And whereas she did not appear to notice them, he had to pause occasionally. "I suffer from a stitch in the side when climbing or walking fast," he explained his pokiness.

"Perhaps Dr. Ulric should see you about it," she commented when she saw the stairs had winded him. "He was no help of course with Gareth, but then the specialists weren't either."

"Mr. De Lakes, I must ask one thing of you . . ." She turned back to face him. "Please don't let him see any extreme emotion on your face . . . If you could sort of look poker-faced even . . . It's hard for him to see outsiders. . . . So we'll go very quietly now and look in on him, for I want you to be his . . ." (he felt, as she stumbled for the word, she had been about to say *keeper*) "companion. I do want you for the post, sir, and I hope you realize this."

She knocked on the door then, and cried out in a voice which had almost a note of awe in it, "It's Mother, Gareth . . . May we come in . . . I'm with the young man who has come to see you. . . ."

Sidney felt a thrill of terror too now, a remembrance of the emotion he had used to feel when Vance visited him in prison.

"Come!" a rather deep but almost childish voice responded.

Mrs. Vaisey opened the big milk-colored door then, and they stood a moment looking into the large dimly lit interior.

A young man about twenty sat in a tall custom-made chair, his hands folded over his lap. For anything there was of expression in them, his eyes might have been made of glass. But his mouth moved convulsively as he took in Vance's brother.

"This is Sidney De Lakes, Gareth, who will be staying with us now. That is if you should wish him to, dearest . . ."

She almost pushed Sidney in the direction of her son.

"Gareth, good morning," he spoke throatily and took the boy's hand and lifted it, heavy as sand, from his lap and held it in his for a moment. The hand then fell back.

"I already know your son, ma'am, you see. From a while back," Sidney managed to explain, but the look of confusion or astonishment on the mother's face struck down whatever more he might have been going to say.

"And I hope we will be good friends again, Gareth," the job-seeker got out, but as he said this facing Mrs. Vaisey she gently moved Sidney's face with her hands back in the direction of her son.

"It had slipped my mind that you two boys used to know one another!" Irene exclaimed as she watched the two young men stare now into one another's faces. Confusion and wonder caused her voice to waver. "I for one," she went on in a soft, almost prayerful voice, "am very happy Mr. De Lakes has agreed to be with us, Gareth, and I can tell by your expression you are also. . . . So," she went on still more nervously as she studied their rapt scrutiny of one another, "we will bid you good morning now, Gareth, dear, until the proper arrangements can be worked out."

"Does the renderer know you're out, Sidney?" the young invalid inquired unexpectedly in clear, loud and almost menacing tones.

Sidney faltered only a moment. "I reckon, Garey, everybody knows I am by now."

"Everybody don't matter, Sid, and you know it. It's him that matters . . ."

"We will not tire you further now, dear," Mrs. Vaisey spoke with her usual cool authority, and bent down and kissed him.

"Mother," Sidney's "charge" now spoke in a kind of panic, "the renderer didn't *send* him to us, did he?"

"Categorically not. Mr. De Lakes came of his own free will, dear . . . Because he knew you, as I have been reminded, and you see, he wished to be with you again . . ." Her voice trailed off and she turned toward the door.

When they were downstairs again, both Mrs. Vaisey and Sidney made no reference to the rather unexpected topic of conversation Gareth had engaged them in, though both of them were, strangely, upset by it.

"Will you tell me my duties, Mrs. Vaisey," Sidney sought to know in the face of her perturbation.

"The simplest," she attempted to rally now, and smiled. "The main thing is merely that you be near him. I had no idea that you had been friends!" She stopped and a frown passed briefly over her face. "But that's all to the good. . . . I don't suppose likewise I should be surprised you both know the renderer. (I wish he would not use that expression with reference to him!)

"Your only duties," she went on now in a manner more like

the composed and slightly regal one with which she had first greeted him, "well, just to sit with him, by the hour if necessary and speak about anything you think would interest him, or, better, anything which would interest you. . . . And try to change the subject when he mentions anybody or anything which agitates him . . ."

"Mrs. Vaisey," he began in a voice that had almost a hint of a wail, "you do understand that I have been in prison."

"I do, I do," she replied. "But if you think that I believe you are . . . like any . . . prisoner" (she winced after having chosen this word), "you are mistaken. I am a great reader of character. I liked you the moment you came in, and you have in me a friend. Dr. Ulric is made of ice water and steel, Mr. De Lakes. . . . But you will find in me a friend who stands firm in time of trial. . . ."

He could think of nothing to say to this, and then they heard her car in the driveway, and the chauffeur honked the horn in rapid resounding summons that recalled a bugle.

She indicated he must take the limousine and was not to walk home under any circumstances.

"I'll expect you then tomorrow for sure!" She took his hand through the open window of the car. "And, oh please," she went on while giving the driver a sign he was to shut off the motor while she spoke. "It would make things easier if we called one another by our Christian names."

"Our Christian names, yes, ma'am," he spoke huskily and extricated his hand from hers.

"Again what a stroke of fortune you already have been friends with Gareth! That was quite unexpected . . ."

"It's good all around . . ."

She smiled and touched his sleeve with her hand.

"It will be something at last to look forward to for him and me." She gave her final goodbye and nodded to the driver to start the motor.

She stood in the middle of the road waving to him as the car drove away in thick clouds of white, ascending dust.

Sidney could tell at once of course that Vance did not like the arrangement at all. At the same time he bombarded his brother with a hundred questions about the "post," as he called it, and the great sprawling house where his duties were to hold him, and about Mrs. Vaisey herself.

"You'll never be able to stand it in the world," Vance finally gave judgment when Sidney had described his "reception."

"But, Vance, God Almighty, it's always you who were telling me I've got to go out and face people ... Now I've gone and done it, you're cross and put out. When even your mentor, Dr. Ulric, is behind my move!"

"Being shut up with a moody, sick boy and his domineering, rich mother is not my idea of getting out and meeting people," Vance snapped. "And you have no training to be a male nurse which is just what you'll be."

"Well thanks, Vance, for your encouragement. . . . At least Irene does not consider that I will be what you call me." His face grew taut with anger.

"So you call her Irene already?" Vance observed.

"I tried, Vance, to tell you a little about some of the things that happened to me in prison. . . . You say I ought to go out and meet people. Maybe my trouble is I have met too many people while you are the one who's never been out in the world and seen what it's like. . . . And you don't want to see I have changed . . . So taking care of a young man won't be hard on me after what I went through. . . ."

"You never liked taking care of me when I was a baby . . . Mother told me how nauseated you got when you had to change my diapers, how fretful and restless you were when she left me alone with you . . ."

"You were a very ill-tempered and irritable brat," Sidney smiled in spite of himself. "Just the way you are now. . . . But, Vance, prison took all the starch out of me . . . Don't you see? And I'll feel I'm doing some good taking care of this boy . . . Besides I used to know him . . ."

As he said this both young men exchanged eloquent looks with one another. The words "the renderer" were on both their lips, for everybody knew that Gareth had also been *his* pupil.

Partly because the stairs had made him realize he was not so robust as he had been when he was a star football player, Sidney had resigned himself to going by limousine to Mrs. Vaisey's, though the stuffiness of both the chauffeur and car made him wish he had walked.

He got more than a little panicky though when he alit from the car and stood before the five-pillared white house. Well, he alibied to himself, one is always a bit nervous on the threshold of a new job. But something else warned him, and he believed his sudden flare-up of "heart-trouble" (which the prison doctor had spoken to him about) had everything to do with the young man with the indefinable ailment whom he was to care for.

"I can't tell you what a weight has been taken off my mind," Irene Vaisey greeted him as she came out on the endless expanse of the porch and, with a glance at the chauffeur, dismissed him. "I've felt positively refreshed, even elated, knowing you will be here to look after him. . . . We won't ask more of you than that, Mr. De Lakes . . ."

Sidney gave her a look of such questioning and uncertain wonder that she turned her eyes away for a moment. She was the first woman he had talked with for, well, he could not remember actually when. His mother—almost that far back.

"Have you had breakfast, Mr. De Lakes?"

"I thought we were to call one another by our . . . first names," he broke out of his bashfulness. "Yes, my brother Vance prepared me a little something as a matter of fact."

"But you could stand with something else, *Sidney*?" She laughed and took his hand. "Certainly a cup of coffee?"

"I'm not supposed to drink any, but actually I would like a cup."

Irene Vaisey rang a small bell whose voice thrilled with a pure silver tone which he had never heard before.

A girl dressed in a highly starched apron and little white-frilled cap entered with a tray on which a solid silver pot of coffee rested, and two plates filled with cornbread and bacon.

"Just taste a little of each, why don't you?" At a motion of her hand they both seated themselves.

"You will think me a fool," she began in a very much altered voice, "when I keep telling you what a burden is lifted by your coming here."

A short sob escaped from her. "Excuse me," she said and reached in a fold of her long dress for a handkerchief. "Gareth's father would have had his heart broken had he lived to see him like this . . . For Gareth was his favorite."

"But he will recover, Mrs. Vaisey . . . Irene," Sidney stretched out his hand toward her, but she did not see it, and he let it fall to his lap.

"You're ready for another cup of coffee, I see," she said after a pause during which she considered his opinion.

"The task I want you to help me with this morning, Sidney, is actually the most difficult one of all. . . . It is to . . . assist him manage his breakfast . . . You see he refuses to eat . . ."

Snatches of Vance's warnings and dark suspicions crossed Sidney's mind.

"I will do most of the task this morning, but if you could from time to time help him . . . chew and swallow just a little of his breakfast . . . It would be a good beginning . . ."

Sidney nodded and tried to look confident.

"I know you're not squeamish," she proceeded. "I know too you have been hurt and you will be able to understand others who have been badly damaged also."

She stood up then and he followed her up the steps.

"You need not go so slow," he spoke directly behind her. "My condition is not that bad."

"Just the same, we won't hurry, Sidney. We have no fixed schedule in this house."

A flood of orange sunlight rushed upon them as they reached the upstairs landing. The door to Gareth's room was wide open, but a curtain of heavy silk hanging between door and room protected the interior from visibility.

Mrs. Vaisey flung back the curtain and motioned Sidney to go in first.

Gareth was seated in the same chair he had been in the previous day. Special care had been made with his grooming, and he wore a jacket and brand-new tie. In his right hand he held a fresh-cut autumn white rose, which it was clear someone had insisted he hold and which he was wanting to get rid of. Mrs. Vaisey took the flower from his fingers and kissed him on the mouth.

"You remember our good friend Sidney, dear."

Gareth moved his head in assent.

A man of about thirty entered the room now with a heavy tray which he deposited on the table beside Gareth, who looked at the man fixedly and then gave him what appeared to be an imperious look of contemptuous dismissal. The servant left without a word.

Irene and Sidney had seated themselves, and had anyone passed through the hall and looked beyond the fluttering curtain he would have thought they were waiting for a service to commence.

"I am sure, Gareth," Mrs. Vaisey broke the silence, "that you are going to be very happy with Sidney. I can feel it, dearest."

Gareth turned his large, luminous eyes on the new "companion."

"Garey," Sidney began, his voice almost bass with strain, "though I have been gone some considerable time and there have been changes in both our lives . . ." He broke off in an excess of emotion. "I will do my best for you, you know that," he managed to finish.

Gareth turned away from both his visitors.

"Shall we begin your breakfast," Mrs. Vaisey's voice also shook, and her eyes rested on the carpet and not on her son. Looking up she saw Gareth shaking his head angrily, and his left hand suddenly disarranged his perfectly tied cravat.

"But you must eat, sweetheart . . . You must keep up your strength . . . And if you are good this morning, Mr. De Lakes will help you also with other things. . . . See what a kind and friendly man he is! He understands our problem, dear, also . . . He has not been immune either . . . to problems . . ."

At that moment Sidney's spine froze for the youth let out a cry like that of a wild animal which feels a bullet graze its skull. Mrs. Vaisey closed her eyes.

"You must and shall eat," she said after a pause, and rose.

The youth shook his head, or what now appeared to Sidney as his mane for with his shock of yellow hair he was so like some forest beast.

"We will not put it on, dear heart, if you will only eat."

Another savage cry came from his throat, which was distended with veins and arteries standing out in clear outlines.

Irene rang, and the servant who had been standing outside returned with a kind of straitjacket, which he quickly and expertly threw over the young man.

Sidney felt faint; ice cold drops of sweat fell from his armpits as they had done in prison. But he was determined to stick it out, he did not wish to return to Vance in failure, and furthermore he wanted somehow to be near this strange troubled boy who did not want food to sustain life.

"Just one piece of bread, that's all you need eat, darling . . . Just one crumb then, see, from my hands . . ."

With consummate skill Mrs. Vaisey forced open her son's mouth and placed on his tongue a piece of bread, and then pushed his jaws shut.

"Chew, Gareth . . . Chew!"

His mouth dripping with saliva, he made a supreme effort to masticate the bread while his wide, terrified eyes roved in the direction of Sidney.

Suddenly he moved his head vigorously toward the new "caretaker."

"You wish Sidney to give you your breakfast?"

Gareth's eyes widened eloquently.

"I believe he wishes you to give him his breakfast," Mrs. Vaisey turned to Sidney.

Sidney rose, and looking at Mrs. Vaisey for encouragement and instruction, he lifted a piece of bread to the boy's mouth. He accepted it and chewed the bread.

"Another, perhaps?" Mrs. Vaisey inquired in a faint voice, hardly that of a whisper.

Sidney had already put another piece of bread in his mouth. He chewed and swallowed this also. Finally a whole slice of bread had been thus laboriously fed to him.

Then as Sidney was withdrawing his hand, the boy took Sidney's index and middle finger and held them with his bared teeth. Mrs. Vaisey immediately went up to the boy, but there was at present no indication of a wish to hurt or bite, he merely held the fingers gently in his mouth. It was Sidney's benign calm attitude which prevented Mrs. Vaisey from doing more at the moment. Indeed she waited as calm and resigned as if she had discovered the two of them at prayer.

Without warning Gareth released his hold on Sidney's fingers, and the new "companion" slipped back away and sat down in a chair which Irene had quickly placed within his reach.

Mrs. Vaisey was busily wiping Gareth's face and mouth free of crumbs and spittle. It was as if she dared not now look at Sidney. Yet finally she did turn from her "charge," and advancing a few steps in the direction of the "caretaker" she addressed him almost in a singing tone: "You are price-less . . . I cannot believe my good fortune if you will only stay . . . I had never dreamed anyone like you would come to us . . . I will always be in your debt."

She then left the room and remained outside the billowing curtain. He barely was listening to her sobs and cries for Gareth was gazing at his new companion with a look of such intense and terrible command that Sidney, deaf now to the happy grief of the mother outside, approached the boy and quickly bending down kissed him on the mouth, a kiss that was as quickly returned.

Sidney came down the endless succession of stairs extremely slowly. Irene Vaisey was waiting at the foot of the staircase, her left hand, which bore an immense yellow stone, was resting on the ancient newel post.

"You look terribly tired, my dear fellow." She spoke in her rather hard dry voice now. The look of worry and concern for him was wonderfully soothing.

"I'm more . . . happy than tired," he told her.

She waited a moment for his remark to settle with her, then replied: "You have every reason to be."

Irene led the way into the dining hall, and from there into a small adjoining alcove. "We'll be more comfortable in here," she explained. "You're positively sure you're all right?" she returned to the subject of his health.

As a matter of fact he was trembling all over, but his health was not the source of his agitation.

She rang a bell (in this house every room had a bell for summoning somebody).

"Will you have some hot chocolate?"

"Oh, anything," he spoke almost deliriously she felt. Then he smiled and this smile meant more to her than anything she had received from anybody in years, as her son's kiss had meant to him.

The maid came again and Mrs. Vaisey issued rather lengthy

instructions, none of which he even heard.

"If you will stay," her voice reached him as if from some parapet, "you will make me the happiest Mother in the world. . . . You don't know what happiness was mine when I saw Gareth took to you at once . . . You see he could never bear anybody except me even to touch him until today. . . . He let you feed him . . . an entire piece of bread! . . . I do believe he would have eaten the entire loaf from your hands."

The girl brought in two trays loaded with a hot chocolate-colored drink, rolls, and tiny silver receptacles of whipped cream by each cup, starched stiff linen napkins, hand-painted china cups. Sidney drank greedily, his mouth stained with the chocolate drink and whipped cream which he consumed separately.

"Whatever you wish in the way of remuneration," she began now on more practical considerations, "ask, simply ask . . . Where he is concerned nothing is too much, don't you agree?"

Then almost without warning, and as in a film where the scene and time sequence change precipitously, and with her voice falling into a low register, she said, "You may or may not know the story of Gareth, but let me tell you to prevent misunderstanding and correct any garbled version you may have listened to. . . . Before our calamity . . ." she had begun, but here the maid had come in to collect the trays and was dismissed by a mere look from her, "we had had no idea Gareth was keeping such bad company, or that he was using, well, a certain drug. We had no inkling of any of that."

Sidney found himself, to his own consternation, breaking almost into a grin, which she may not have seen, for she went ahead with what she wished him to know: "His father and his two twin brothers were going to get the new horse from the stables over in Virginia. Gareth was the best driver, you may know, and of course he was the oldest of my sons . . ."

"Who were his bad company, ma'am, may I inquire?" Sidney interrupted. She paused only long enough to ignore his question, and continued:

"I begged them not to go that day. All their horoscopes were bad in the newspaper, for one thing. I told them I would drive. They paid no attention to me, Sidney. None whatsoever. . . . It happened at high noon. Gareth had been smoking this drug his friends had been giving him. But he must have seen the train coming, nonetheless, grass or no grass . . . How could he have failed to?"

She stopped and looked at his mouth, perhaps to see if it moved in the strange smile she had caught him in before.

"But I'm a bit ahead of my story. . . . The actual wreck was caused, a witness claims, by a race. Yes, that is correct, a race. A young man riding a horse, according to this observer, passed our truck several times, and the rider is said to have taunted Gareth, shouted abuse at him, and dared him to race him to the train crossing. Another motorist also later told me the same story, but he refused nonetheless to appear at the inquest. (I disremember his name too after all this time.) 'Let's race, Garey! Let's beat the train!' the horseman is said to have exclaimed. 'I'll race you to the train tracks and beat you . . . Will you race me,' he kept calling, *'or are you chicken?'* And so they raced, Sidney, raced the train. And the horseback rider got across the tracks in time, and won the race, and me and mine you see did not . . ."

"But who was this . . . rider?" Sidney wondered, absorbed in her account.

Irene sat for a while in deep silence. He was about to repeat his question when she replied: "We never found out. . . . Indeed now Gareth claims he does not remember any 'race' or any 'rider.'"

Sidney looked away from her despairing and anguished face.

"There may be many trying things for you, Sidney," she began again, "should you decide to take this responsibility upon your shoulders . . . I do not want to mitigate the fact that there may be unpleasantness, and rather a lot of it. Even when he was . . . himself, he was a difficult, headstrong, and, yes, passionate boy."

She watched him drink the hot beverage and eat a large sweet roll heaped with strawberry glaze. He ate, she realized, in order to have something to do, not through appetite.

"You talk as if I was Vance," he finally spoke with a full mouth, and with a trace of anger in his speech. "As I tried to tell him, prison had everything. They gave me many gifts, Mrs. Vaisey" (he fell away again from using her Christian name). "I'm broken, I guess. They broke me . . . But I can do all you expect or Gareth expects partly because I guess I am broken."

"You are not broken, Sidney. You are perfect."

He shook his head dubiously, but again he smiled.

"Then I can expect everything of you?" She sounded, he thought, almost like a conspirator.

"Absolutely," he replied at once. "Where he is concerned —where you are concerned—everything."

"As I said before," she thanked him with her eyes, "it's more than I could ever have hoped for."

She picked up her own cup of the chocolate mixture for the first time, brought it to her mouth, and without having tasted it, put it down again noiselessly.

"Do you think later on, Sidney, you might even stay day and night? . . . Take up your residence here, that is . . ."

He hesitated. "I don't know what Vance would say to that . . . Night and day . . . You see I owe him so much. It was him got me out of prison . . . He went to the Governor . . ."

"I know," Mrs. Vaisey said coldly. "But Vance has Dr. Ulric . . . Doesn't he?" she added, at a look of confusion from the "caretaker."

"But it is right," she continued, "to begin even more slowly with you, Sidney, than we did with the others who took care of Gareth . . . They were after all not 'called' to be in charge of him . . . So we will expect you then only during the day for the time being . . . After that we shall see . . ."

He offered to leave then by rising, and she put her hand on his sleeve.

"Never doubt me, Sidney," she gave him her last word then.

"My back was to the wall until Sidney came."
Irene Vaisey had confided this sentiment to a yellowing mass of papers which a more ordinary woman might have called her diary. (A lengthy description of the De Lakes boy followed in her fine meticulous hand.)

"What will Vance say about my hands?" Sidney wondered aloud as he was being driven home so that the chauffeur, who was not sure he had heard the question correctly, asked him to repeat it.

Sidney's hands were covered with teeth marks.

"You need not keep your hands hidden, Sidney," Vance had said as they were finishing their supper that evening. "I noticed them at once."

"I belong there, Vance," his brother raised his voice edgily. "Both Mrs. Vaisey and I are in the same boat, if you ask me."

Vance put down his knife and fork with a bang.

"All right, then," Sidney began shamefacedly. "My hands are bitten from when I feed Gareth . . . He can't feed himself . . ."

A look of almost lordly disgust came over Vance's flushed face.

"Look, Vance . . . It's what I want to do . . . It quiets me down . . ."

"Getting bit quiets you down?"

"I'm helping someone."

"Does he know you're helping. Does he know anything? I ask you. Of course he doesn't. You might as well feed a corpse . . ."

"Vance, don't say anymore. . . . I think you are angry with me really because I told you I was . . . that way . . ."

"I'm not at all," Vance interrupted him passionately. "I don't believe you're queer anyhow, or gay, or whatever they call it . . . Prison made you think that . . ."

"Oh, Vance, Vance . . . I am, I am, I am."

Suddenly Sidney sobbed and put his hands over his eyes so that the bite marks at last were clearly put up for show.

Vance excused himself, took his plate, and walked to the kitchen. He let the water faucet run full force so that he would not hear anything from the dining room.

When he reentered the room, Sidney had taken his hands down from his eyes and was looking blindly at his bread pudding which had been made that day by Dr. Ulric's cook.

41

"Sidney, it's all right," Vance said, and went over to his brother and put his hand on his shoulder. "Forgive my bad temper."

"It's the only thing I'm good for, Vance . . . To feed a dead boy."

At this Vance turned his own face away, and pressed his fingers hard into Sidney's shoulder, allowing finally his hand to rest there.

Irene was waiting for him the next day, dressed in a billowing gauzelike gown with little blue flowers designed all over it, and a kind of satin bow round her narrow waist. A perfume almost like that of peonies came bearing down upon Sidney as he took her hand.

"I thought if you would care to I would show you a film I made of Garey just two years ago . . . It takes only a few minutes . . . Would you want to see it, Sidney?"

"Oh, you know me, you know I do."

There were times when she looked extraordinarily like her son. It was uncanny.

They went immediately into a small room which adjoined the rather oversumptuous—but forlorn from disuse—parlor, and Irene beckoned him to come sit in a mammoth flowered upholstered chair. She had already set up the projector, and she called now for the servant who seemed always to be waiting nearby for her summons. His name was Damon. He almost never showed any emotion, interest or even indication he saw or recognized anybody. Damon immediately adjusted the projector, and the single word, in black-purplish letters,

GARETH

streamed across the somewhat oval-shaped screen which Sidney had not at first observed against the back wall.

Mrs. Vaisey sat directly behind him on a kind of camp stool. Sidney was not certain whether Damon had left the room or not. He suspected he had not, but turned his head, was smiled at by Irene, and then caught a glimpse of Damon working the projector with contemptuous competence.

There was first a picture of the "former" Gareth in the horse stables, currying a white gelding spotted with gold markings. Next one saw him riding another more-spirited horse about the track which was about a mile or more from the Vaisey house. There was a close-up finally of Gareth standing with his one hand holding the reins and his other forming a tightly clenched fist. It was this close-up which struck a kind of desperate unease in Sidney. The handsome boyish face, certainly full of health and even good humor, nonetheless had something in it—perhaps the expression lay in his mouth—which hinted at, what was it? Disaster probably. The disaster which Sidney knew had overtaken him, and which perhaps he was after all reading into the film itself. No, he thought, disaster still to come, and he shivered.

Then one caught a view of Gareth sitting alone near a haystack. Evening was falling; and since the film now unexpectedly had sound, one could hear the distant baying of dogs and then, almost as though the real Gareth, that is the Gareth upstairs, had suddenly decided to attend his own showing, one heard his speaking voice. However what he said was so garbled and unconnected with anything he was doing or which the film had shown before that Sidney, in extreme discomfiture, half rose, and then remembering where he was as quickly sat down. Gareth said:

I promised to meet him over near Warrior Creek, but my horse never liked to go that far for some reason. So I finally had to go on foot. The creek had gone dry though, and I wasn't sure I had reached the right place after all. But he was waiting for me all right, and he said he would have waited if necessary till the ice caps had melted and the mountains turned to dust.

There was a great deal of noise now like static on the sound track, and though Gareth went on speaking one heard nothing more audible from him.

"Where is Warrior Creek, ma'am?" Sidney inquired, looking behind him, but Irene had her head down in her hands and evidently either did not hear him or was too upset to reply.

Then came a final shot of Gareth with his then rather long curly hair blowing in the considerable wind, with a merging close-up of his eyes and forehead, both now serene. His mouth came open at the very end, but no sound emerged. But he had said something, and Sidney tried to form the lines of his own lips as he had seen Gareth do in order to refashion what he had pronounced. He had no success.

Damon turned on the lights, and Irene was smiling now.

They left the room together. The perfume of the peonies had vanished, and all around them one could inhale now a kind of strong leather odor, as though the reins and the bridle and the saddle depicted in the film had been brought into the room and set down somewhere. Outside too one heard dogs barking vociferously.

"He's a bit under the weather today, so that I thought we would not ask you to go upstairs, Sidney . . ."

Vance's brother showed such deep disappointment that she went on:

"Unless of course you do wish to."

"I do." He spoke to his own surprise in a kind of rude, loud, almost angry tone.

"I didn't quite feel you should have to do what has to be done today. And which Damon is quite prepared to do until you are a bit more settled."

"But I thought," Sidney kept the angry tone in his voice predominant, "that I was to learn everything from the outset.... Have you had second thoughts about me, Mrs. Vaisey?"

"Please say Irene."

He was silent.

"Second thoughts, never," she spoke like one injured, and her gaze moved toward the upstairs. "But the task we have to do now is so unpleasant," she defended her position.

"Then I welcome the unpleasantness, ma'am."

She looked at him with considerable wonder.

"Did the film . . . help you in any way?" she inquired, like one who is stalling for time.

"He was, and he is a wonderful young man. . . . He rides like . . . he was the air itself, like . . . a spirit," he concluded painfully. He had been going to say like a *god,* but he was shamed or timid of his great admiration for his charge.

"He won a good many awards at the rodeo," the mother spoke with a kind of indifference now like one reading by request a newspaper write-up.

"What task then is so unpleasant for me," he chided her.

She waited some while. "His bowels haven't moved for several days," Irene said at last sharply. "Usually Damon and I . . ."

"No," Sidney began, and at the same time he felt frightened at his own vigorous eagerness, "you should trust him to me . . . I mean I am the one to do it, Irene. It's my duty, as he is my charge now . . ."

"But he isn't perhaps quite at ease with you yet . . . I'm so troubled he . . . put his teeth on you."

"No, no, don't you see," he tried to keep down his own eloquence, "it was after all not meant to hurt me . . . I'm glad in fact that . . ."

"Let us sit on a little before we go up," Irene suggested now in the face of his growing eagerness.

"As you wish. Of course."

They went into the interior now of the parlor and took seats directly in front of one another in two heavy wooden chairs with sharp brass ornaments adorning their tops.

She began again: "It's a very trying thing to get his bowels to move now." She forced these words out. "He nearly died last winter. They feared in fact obstruction. . . . He neither wants to eat . . . or to void." She used this "hospital" word in some dismay, unclear as to what word might be appropriate for Sidney.

"He will be better under my care," he spoke almost boastfully.

"I am sure of that, Sidney."

Gareth was standing when they entered his room. He at once rushed toward Sidney and placed himself protectively behind the latter, and then cried out in his hoarse animal-like voice, but this time framing the voice into words: "Don't let her touch me, keep her away!"

"Gareth, Gareth!" came the anguished but also now angry voice of his mother, while Sidney had to call into question his own recollection, for he had thought Gareth never spoke, and now he had spoken as clear as could be, although the actual sound of the words themselves were so little like that of a human being, quivers went again up and down his spine.

Sidney held his charge's hand, and could feel the rapid pulse coming and going under his fingertips.

"Gareth, listen to me," she began again. "The only reason we hurt you the last time was because we were too nervous, too afraid in fact of hurting you. . . . Today, Sidney will do it all for you . . . If you will only allow him to, I know that in his hands you will feel no pain . . . So please, my dear . . ."

Meanwhile Mrs. Vaisey had spread out thick sheets over the bed, had pulled out a chamberpot of huge size from under it, and a tube of salve, and an enema apparatus.

Gareth emerged now from behind Sidney's protection, and stared at the ongoing preparations.

"I have already gone to the bathroom, Mother, and you know it," he spoke clearly and collectedly.

"Then this will be no trouble for you at all," she replied. "Sidney will help you take off your clothing."

Mrs. Vaisey had to call Sidney to attention, for his thoughts were far away, that is as far as prison. He felt he was about to inflict on this boy who appeared so trapped and helpless what the prisoners, the serious criminals, had so often inflicted on him so many times in the toilet and the shower and which he had wanted to tell Vance about, but Vance, who always appeared white-robed and immaculate, as in a church choir, had forbidden him to speak.

"Sidney!" Mrs. Vaisey's concerned voice, coming, it seemed, from miles away, brought him back to the present. "What is it, Sidney . . . ?"

She had come over to him and put her arm about him. "I can take over, you know," she spoke more soothingly to him

47

than she had to her son. "You look so distressed . . ."

"No whispering over there at my expense!" Gareth's angry voice rose from the bed, where he lay completely disrobed by his own hands.

"Perhaps if you left the room, Mrs. Vaisey, it would be better this time . . ."

She gave Sidney a peculiar searching look. She turned her eyes slowly to Gareth, then gave one last glance at Sidney, and went out the door. But she returned almost immediately. "The warm water is here," she pointed to a huge basin sitting on a table, "ready to be put in the bag. I'll remain directly outside should anything more be needed."

"I would just go downstairs if I were you," Sidney advised her. He was entirely in possession of himself now.

"Very well, then, if you say so," she agreed. She avoided looking at Gareth again.

Sidney waited until he heard her footsteps descending the stairs.

"Now then, Gareth, you won't mind me, I know." He put his hand on the sufferer's forehead.

"Hands like a cake of ice," Gareth remarked as he watched the new "caretaker" with dilated pupils.

Sidney rubbed his hands vigorously to warm them while never taking his eyes off his charge.

"Now let me, Garey, and don't fight it." As he said this his lips almost grazed those of the patient. "Turn over and we'll soon be done." Gareth flopped over petulantly.

As he inserted the tube in him, Gareth responded with angry beastlike cries and clenched and gnashed his teeth. A cold sweat had broken all over his back and he shivered almost like a person in a paroxysm.

48

"Tell me when you've taken all the warm water you can ... Gareth, do you mind me? ... Tell me when you can't hold no more."

Sidney could not resist touching his lips to the firm pink pair of buttocks, which caused his charge to thrash angrily and as a result the tube caused him pain. He howled.

"You hold that in until you can't take any more now," Sidney spoke sharply.

A lengthy silence followed.

"Then, *now*, for cripes sake, now, you idiot, pull it out now!" Gareth scolded viciously. Sidney pulled out the tube as gently as possible and picking him up bodily he carried him to the chamber pot and held him down on it.

Gareth shot looks of fury, humiliation, grief and even sardonic humor with his new attendant, and then as the sounds of his bowels loosening filled the room, he shouted:

"I will get even if it takes me a hundred years!"

Looking down into the pot, after Gareth had risen and Sidney was wiping him with—at Irene's special insistence— a very expensive thin linen cloth, he saw that what had come out of the boy was flecked with blood.

"Gareth," Sidney pointed to this.

"Clothe me," his charge said in sullen contempt, "and be quick about it."

He was putting his socks on last when Gareth pulled his feet loose hastily and said, "Why don't you lick my toes for a stretch, go on ... Go on, I won't tell on you, murderer ..."

Sidney blinked, coughed, and then his mouth fell over the toes, which had an odor about them like preserved cherries.

After a few moments of these caresses Gareth kicked him violently away.

"No brother of mine is going to empty used chamber pots!"

Vance had hurled this statement at Sidney as his last word on the subject during their two-hour bickering and quarreling over "everything," and then had rushed out the door, and driven off in Dr. Ulric's new car.

It had never occurred to Sidney that his brother would go straight to Mrs. Vaisey's house.

Vance had never known himself to be so angry, but he knew from some experience of his flying off the handle in the past that it would have been wiser to have waited until morning before taking any "action"; and even as he was ringing the doorbell—it was ten-thirty at night—he realized he was probably making a bad mistake.

Late as it was, Mrs. Vaisey was only just then taking her supper, seated alone at the end of an eighteen-foot dining table illuminated now only by a single tall drooping white candle. She did not rise or, indeed, speak when Vance was ushered in by Peter Damon, who had announced the visitor's name and that the purpose of his visit was urgent.

"Sidney is all right, I hope," she greeted him with alarm, for she could only construe his coming as being dictated by bad news.

When her visitor still failed to speak, she rose:

"There's nothing seriously wrong, is there?"

"I had no idea you would be dining, Mrs. Vaisey. . . . You'll have to forgive me coming so late too . . . I will leave and return." He moved toward the door.

"But what is your news?" She was convinced by now something terrible had happened to her new "hope."

"I have no news, I'm afraid." His anger, his courage, and his belief in his own mission had all but collapsed in the face of his meeting with his "enemy." He slumped unbidden into a chair.

"I dine late," she told him. A self-deprecating smile passed over her lips and, seating herself again and drinking hastily from a glass of white wine, "Because this is almost the only hour in the entire twenty-four that is free from hustle and bustle, confusion, and even terror. . . . Do please remain seated" (he had risen as she said this). "Can't I offer you something to eat or drink . . . ?"

"No, no, please," Vance began while she studied his face anxiously trying to see if there was any resemblance between the brothers, and finding to her disappointment very little if any, for Vance had fair hair and brown eyes, and there was a certain smug and satisfied look about his mouth and brow.

"My brother and I have had a terrible row, Mrs. Vaisey. We almost came to blows . . . I may as well tell you, I do not approve of his being . . . a drudge."

"Indeed," she stared at him loftily. "Does he think so poorly then of his position here."

"Quite the contrary . . . He is disgustingly happy here, I'm afraid."

"Why be afraid then of happiness?" A wave of triumph suffused her features, which the flickering light from the candle emphasized.

"But it is the wrong kind of happiness, Mrs. Vaisey, don't you see."

"Isn't happiness always just happiness, Mr. De Lakes . . . Unless happiness itself is a sin."

He smiled in spite of himself.

"Let us go into the parlor and talk, for I can see you are very upset, and I have no appetite at all tonight . . . Have been sitting here staring at my plate for what seems hours . . . Come on, please, shall we?"

She took him by the hand and led him into the spacious adjoining room.

"You'll have some after-dinner coffee at least," she proposed, and her visitor nodded.

His anger had gone, but he still felt compelled to get Sidney released. He must not empty slop jars!

"You should realize that what your brother has accomplished for my son is far greater than any specialist or doctor could or did achieve. So that your fear Sidney is in a demeaning kind of position can't stand scrutiny, Mr. De Lakes . . . And I am prepared to pay him a fee as high as that of any specialist . . . Don't you see, he is changing our whole life here. . . ."

He found his own argument cut from under him and was bereft all at once both of a rejoinder and a mission.

"All that I feared," he was now all apology, "is that his life here would continue what he calls the shame and humiliation of his prison experiences, where I fear he lost a great deal of his self-respect and dignity, his belief in himself. . . . He says, Mrs. Vaisey, that 'terrible things' happened to him behind bars . . . I have not listened to what happened because I felt it would not be to either of our advantages."

"Advantage?" She was shocked by the use of this word. She scowled, then went on:

"But don't you think you should have listened?" she asked with some heat. "After all to whom could he turn but his own brother . . . I mean after all whom could he unburden himself to but you?"

Vance stared at her lengthily.

"He did not ask to be unburdened," he went on. "He simply told me prison had . . . well . . . unmanned him I think the word was . . . That he had been *used.*"

The last word had slipped out without his wishing it to, and immediately he had betrayed to her how much more he was leaving out in the background of their quarrel.

"There!" she cried. "You see he does need someone to unburden to . . . And you are the one naturally he must go to . . . Of course . . ."

"But I feel, you see," he made a last attempt now to get her to understand his point and the meaning of his call, "that if he goes on working here, though he is happy, you say, in his post, it will only add to his feeling of . . ."

". . . being used!" Mrs. Vaisey immediately poured him a cup of coffee on saying this and handed it to him.

"To tell the truth, Mrs. Vaisey, I don't know what I think now."

He was close to tears.

"I don't suppose for a minute that Sidney thinks he will be in what you call his 'post' forever," Mrs. Vaisey went on. "But there is one person I am afraid who expects him to stay forever . . ."

"I see," Vance could barely get these words out.

"Gareth expects him to remain permanently."

A look of blinding displeasure crossed Vance's face.

"Their relationship is that successful?" he inquired huskily.

"I've never seen a relationship . . . so beautiful," she triumphed over him now. "Your brother has already worked a miracle on the boy . . . Gareth was dying until Sidney came."

All Vance's planned speech, argument, his fulmination and judgment were ground to powder by this statement.

"I think it would be a crime now to keep them apart!" she

pressed even further now, although she saw her enemy was crushed.

"But," she went on from the height of her advantage, "I think I could let my own boy die if I thought that his happiness and well-being were earned at the expense of another human being's humiliation . . . or his being used. Yes, I could easily let him die. . . . But you see you are wrong . . . Neither of these two young men feel they are being humiliated or used by needing one another . . ."

"Needing one another!" Vance's earlier anger had turned suddenly to outrage.

"Why do you think Gareth has suddenly found his speech? None of his other 'attendants' restored it to him! And haven't you noticed a change in your brother too?"

Vance bowed his head.

"Mr. De Lakes, answer me."

"Yes, yes." He clenched his fists and simultaneously two tears stood in his eyes.

"I'm sorry," Mrs. Vaisey quieted down, "if we have been quarreling."

"Why shouldn't we quarrel? . . . After all I spent nearly five years trying to get my brother to come home to me, only to lose him to . . ."

". . . a mindless invalid! Isn't that what you're thinking?" She rose.

"I did not say that, Mrs. Vaisey . . . Please excuse me . . ." He unconsciously extended his two hands toward her.

"Sidney may leave any time he wishes . . . Nobody is forcing him to remain here . . ."

A sudden fear now came over Vance that Sidney might lose his place with Gareth. His whole earlier position seemed about to be reversed, and his fear made him stutter badly before he could get out:

"I have only come here because I want the best for Sidney."

"I understand . . . But you will forgive me if I say that in Gareth he has found just that."

Vance came to his feet. His mouth struggling with a whole army of words which he resolutely refused to release.

"We will leave everything just the way it is," he said at last, "and part friends, then?"

She took his hands then in hers, and held them firmly in assent.

One afternoon, a week or so after Vance's unsuccessful visit, Mrs. Vaisey, full of gloomy thoughts, absent-minded and hardly knowing what she was doing, had come noiselessly upstairs. The door to Gareth's room was open and the great billowing curtain, like one of her mother's old brocade dresses, was fluttering in the pre-twilight breeze. She looked within. She was as unprepared for the sight which met her eyes as she would have been to see her own face and form in her casket. Without knowing she was doing so, she entered the room.

Both Gareth and Sidney were naked, holding one another in furious embrace, their bodies covered with their mutual saliva from their kisses, each holding the sex of the other in open, abandoned, furiously moving mouths. Their immoderate pleasure, their almost unconscious bliss made them for some time unaware she stood there. It was Sidney who first loosened his hold on her son, but Gareth went on with his famished caressing of Sidney's body.

"Ma'am," Sidney said at last. "Irene . . ." He gave a frozen idiotic smile.

She had the strength to get out of the room without falling, the ability somehow to walk down the stairs, and into her private writing room. She closed and locked the door. The passage of time seemed endless to her. She barely thought, she did not weep, she was mindless as a stunned bird. She had grown up, she realized, despite her marriage, and her having been educated at fashionable colleges, having studied Greek and French, ignorant of men, ignorant too of women, ignorant of life. She understood though now Vance's "mission."

She had just enough self-knowledge also to realize that it was her jealousy and envy which were making her so sick at this moment.

Then she heard the knock. It could be only one person.

She admired Sidney's manner. He had dressed almost formally, and was wearing one of her son's neckties, which irritated her.

"Mrs. Vaisey," he began, as she rose and greeted him with a cold nod. "I suppose you wish me to leave . . ."

"I never told you, Sidney, that your brother was here a week ago."

"Vance came here?"

"Evidently he knows you better than I do . . ."

She sat down at her spinet desk and began writing out a check. She handed it to him.

"What is this?" he cried on seeing the excessive amount of the denomination. "I won't take it," he said, handing it back to her.

"You have deceived me," she spoke tunelessly and without expression.

"No, ma'am, I have not," he replied. "I'm not ashamed of

love, either, though," he told her, both decisive and faltering in his speech.

"Love?" she thundered now at him.

"Yes," he replied, and offered to go.

"Wait a moment," she said, but as the gnarled old ancient clock ticked away in the study, she could think of nothing to utter. "Very well, then . . ." she was able to say, "the less spoken the better . . ."

"And *he's* better because of what is between us, Mrs. Vaisey . . . Do you hear? I won't share your and Vance's views on it . . . I'll be damned if I will . . . You'll see."

He went out.

She swallowed one of the strong capsules Dr. Ulric had prescribed for her when under stress, then she walked with the little force she could summon up the sixty steps or so to her boy's room. The door was shut as if hammered closed. She knocked. There was no answer. She rapped again, then pressed open the door a small crack. "May I come in, Gareth?" As there was no answer, she opened the door wide and stood on the threshold.

Gareth sat in his best suit, with a silver cravat she had never seen him wear before, his hands folded, appearing much the way he had the time Sidney had made his first appearance.

"Are you all right?" she wondered, going over to him and touching his right hand. "Gareth, will you please speak to Mother?"

His eyes had no more expression than those of a doll, and she wondered if he breathed or could move.

"Gareth, Gareth, do not do this to one who loves you best . . . I can't bear your terrible silence. I know you do it to punish me. I know you hear me. . . . Gareth, I had to send him away. . . . Why do you not speak to me? Haven't I given you my own life, sacrificed all for you . . . Oh, Gareth . . ."

She felt that at least on his lips there was some semblance of life, and though she could detect no movement on them, she felt an expression of both scorn and venom issuing therefrom, so that she winced as if struck by a corrosive liquid.

Then seeing it was useless to remain with one who was again prepared to live as dead, she went shaken and bent out from his room.

Behind this story so far is another story, as behind the girders of an ancient bridge is the skeleton of a child which superstition says keeps the bridge standing.

Sidney had told his brother Vance that he was queer and loved men, but he could never have begun to tell him about the son of the renderer, or the scissors-grinder as he was even more commonly called; he certainly could never have made Vance believe that the "renderer" had been dictating his life from at least the time of the eighth grade on. For Roy had had his eyes on Sidney that long. And he had marked Sidney for his own since then. Sidney knew it, had resisted it, and thereby tightened the cord about both of them. It was Roy Sturtevant, after all, who had sent Brian McFee to him, and then, when this plan had worked out all it was supposed to, he had, angered at the fact they had fallen in love with one another, commanded Brian to shoot Sidney, while meantime having suggested to Sidney by means of an unsigned note that Brian would soon try to kill him somewhere near the Bent Ridge Tavern.

No, it was not surprising that Sidney had not told his brother such a secret. It was too big a secret for one man to tell another and be believed.

But in their constant wrangling and arguing, one statement would come from Sidney again and again, "I tell you I'm afraid of Roy Sturtevant."

"A big strapping fellow like you fear him!"

"All right, Vance . . . No use talking to you then . . ."

But when Mrs. Vaisey had allowed Sidney to leave her service, he found he had nowhere to go. The very thought of returning to Vance and telling him the circumstances of his having lost "the only job he had ever wanted" was insupportable. Neither could he go to Dr. Ulric.

It was then that the chilling awareness came over him that he could go only to one person, his enemy. And at that moment it did not seem too strange to him that he could go confess to the renderer his failing and predicament, rather than Vance; as in prison he had found to his own queer wonder he was more comfortable at last in the company of hardened murderers than with psychiatrists and clergymen.

It was better to eat humble pie with Roy Sturtevant than face Vance's pure and noble wrath and bloodless judging forgiveness.

He had begun, nonetheless, spending the night in the open, but August is cold in the mountains and frost not uncommon, and after lying down for a few hours in a meadow that is not too far from the cemetery, aching and shivering, he started over toward Roy's place, thinking bitterly how his enemy might treat him more kindly in the face of this new disgrace than his own brother.

So when Roy Sturtevant had looked up from sewing on a button on his pants pocket, which had come off endangering his losing his money, and saw the man who had given him no peace since he had fallen in love with him as a boy of fourteen in the eighth grade, he realized all over again what he had always known, that the one who had been in jail all those years was himself, the "scissors-grinder," and not Sidney. He was not sorry Sidney had killed little Brian McFee, not at all, he was glad to be rid of a young man who had wanted to go on by his side for the rest of his life. For imagine having somebody beside you day and night loving you and forgiving you and petting you forever and ever, that must be a better description of hell than being put into a boiling lake or cauldron of ice that burnt you black. So reckoned the scissors-grinder.

But as long as Sid was in jail, he felt all right for he was safe in jail with him, so to speak, for that is what he felt, they were both imprisoned together, and so he had felt good, but now that Sid was out and free, forgiven by everybody, and what is worse installed in Mrs. Vaisey's mansion, all his old sorrow and responsibility and hell were to begin all over again, for he knew as he had known ever since they had set eyes on one another, though from such different social backgrounds, that Sidney now as he had when they had met in the seventh or eighth grade, Sidney was waiting for him to command him again. He did not want to command any more boys, but Sidney would require him to.

"So you have come back then," Roy said at last, having sewed the button on almost too tight to go through the hole.

"I've lost my place at Mrs. Vaisey's." Sidney sat down on the furthest chair away from his host.

"I wondered how long that would last. What did you do wrong this time?"

Every time he looked at Sidney's mouth and wanted to kiss

it of course he saw something written on the mouth which stopped him from pressing his lips at once against Sid's, for the lips appeared to be forming the words all over again *Command me, I am waiting for your orders.*

Roy did not know yet what the orders were this time, that was what made him angry all over again. But he knew Sidney had not been punished enough for all the years he had mistreated him with his sullen and constant tempting him in school, while every so often yielding to him in some dark corridor, or isolated stretch of country woods, only to have this followed by more refusal to speak to him when other boys were present, often cutting him in the halls or on the street, and finally his last refusal to shake hands with him on the night of the high school graduation exercises, when it was Roy who was valedictorian, and treating him to a slap in the face when he had attempted to force Sidney to shake his hand.

His being the son of the renderer and a scissors-grinder, his having risen first as valedictorian of his class and then later becoming through indefatigable labor and sacrifice richer than old Doc Ulric or Mrs. Vaisey or the snots of the De Lakes brothers, nothing of any of his accomplishments made him content or confident. Something was burning in his veins, having its origin perhaps from even before birth, and now it was the sight of Sidney De Lakes which made the fire burn again in his blood. He was glad his blood was burning, for all the time Sidney had been in jail he had been dormant, cold, lifeless clay. He could be himself in any case only when he hated, when he plotted murder, or, better, when he commanded others to murder.

"She caught me touching Gareth."

That was the only sentence in many sentences coming from

a usually laconic (near illiterate, when the truth is told) Sid De Lakes which his ears had picked up, immersed as he was in his own cogitations.

The sound of the name *Gareth* was enough to set his plan formulating. For he knew all at once he could get Sidney again through the Vaisey boy. And this time his plan must work, and Sidney must be crossed off.

"And supposin' I was to go to Mrs. Vaisey and get you took back," the renderer said, putting his needle and thread away in a fancy genuine-leather box and snapping the lid shut with a sharp little bang.

The expression on Sid's face maddened him for it said, *Would she even open the door on your kind?*

"You forget," Roy answered that look of his, "that I taught Gareth how to ride . . ."

"And race to his ruin and the death of his brothers and Dad."

"She complained about that, did she?"

"She only told it."

"She only told her half of the story . . . What about my half, huh?"

Sid put his face in his hands and leaned over low, almost to his boots.

"Fuck my half, is that what you mean by sticking your face inside your palms. . . . He hounded me to race from sunup to sundown. How did I know there was a train, it never even whistled. I don't live over there with the quality and don't know trains . . . Only," he added, "I didn't race Gareth. Brian did."

Sidney took his face out of his hands and looked the renderer straight in the eye and said deep in his throat: "You think

you could manage to have her take me back . . . ? Well, say
so if you can do so . . ."

The renderer nodded deliberately and again and again like
the pendulum of a clock.

"What will I get out of it, Mr. De Lakes?"

"Ain't you got my life already, Roy. I'm where I am today
on account of you."

"Ho, hear him . . . Here we go again now. . . . 'Cause I got
tired of Brian McFee, and give him to you, and you killed him
after an argument . . ."

"You killed both of us . . . Well, stare at me, why don't you.
You know you did. I'm a dead man."

The renderer began rolling some grass in a paper he took
from another little box. It didn't take him long. Sidney pretended he was not observing him, but he couldn't ignore
Roy's putting the lighted reefer in his mouth.

"Calm down now, Sid, I'll get your pretty boy back for
you."

Sidney took a draw of the pot. Two tears streamed down
his face.

"So you don't deny you're in love with Gareth, do you
. . . I know your type. It was me put old Doc Ulric wise as to
there bein' a need of a new caretaker . . . Gareth's an even
bigger snot than you ever was. Of course his mother is from
richer ancestors than your sort of no-account gentry folks
was . . ."

"Thanks, Roy, thanks," Sidney spoke bitterly and hope-
lessly.

"I love you just the same as I did when I was in junior high
school, and was crazy enough to admit it to you then . . ."

"Go ahead blame me, why don't you, for inventing the

world . . . Go on, why don't you . . . I get blamed for the sun going down at night and waking folks up in the morning. Go on, heap it on."

"How much do you love this Gareth?"

"Oh, Roy, shit." After a moment, though, he said, "A lot."

"Then I'll go over and talk to the old lady and see if you'll have your post back . . . And then you can think about payin' me something a little later."

"I bet."

"Thank me, Sid."

"Give me some more of your smoke, why don't you," Sid said.

Going up to his guest, he pushed the grass vigorously into his mouth.

"You weren't never grateful for anything in your life . . . Even your bad luck has been handed to you and you didn't deserve it. Even your murder was done for you. . . . But you will be mine yet, do you hear . . ."

"Yeah," Sid replied, smoking greedily on the grass and trying, it did seem, to finish it all before sharing any of it again, "I heard you from the beginning. . . . All right, get Gareth back, and you can have me later on."

"Will you shake on that, prisoner?"

Sidney gave him a look he had never given any other human being before, but Roy, though hesitating a moment at such fury, took his hand from him and held it in his in a kind of poorly controlled vehemence.

Roy put on his old hunting jacket and pulled on his boots. Sidney also rose as he saw his host going toward the door.

"You wait here now," he told Sidney. "And you wait till I come back, you hear. If she don't take you back, well, you can't very well go home to Vance fired, can you? And if she does take you back, I'll drive you right over to your . . . Well, what *do* you call him, did you say?"

But this time the look on his guest's face made even him stop.

"Just to make sure you don't light out, I will lock this door with a double lock. The sound ought to be familiar," he added.

Alone in the renderer's house, it was as though he was living all over again his life up until he had shot and killed Brian McFee. That is everywhere he looked now he saw, or thought he heard or smelled Brian, who had after all begun by being Roy's friend, Roy's boy.

"I have wrote my name in hell," Brian McFee had said as he was dying on the sawdust of the floor in the Bent Ridge Tavern. The Doc had heard that sentence but had never repeated it to anybody, but Sidney had heard it too, and it came to him again now as clear and audible as if he was back in the time of the events which had led up to these last words of another boy he had thought he had loved.

But before the Doc got there Brian McFee had cried out, even though he had his own gun still smoking as a result of his having fired at Sidney several times in the woods, having tried to kill him there, and Sidney had rushed into the Bent Ridge Tavern hardly knowing what he was doing, and it was then Brian's gun had fallen on the floor, and he had looked into the muzzle of Sidney's leveled gun and shouted:

"Don't shoot me, Sidney, I love you."

He had shot him right through the words that still haunted him today, the most perfect words ever said to him.

"I don't know why I shot him," he had once told the prison psychiatrist, "because after all his gun lay nearly empty on the sawdust . . ."

"I am guilty of murder, not manslaughter," Sidney had told this doc. *"I must find my punishment . . . When I go home I will go to the renderer. . . ."*

"Who is the renderer?" the prison doc had inquired.

"A renderer is what we country jakes call a man who collects carcasses and puts them in boiling water until they are rendered into lard which he makes into soap for people's hands . . ."

"I asked who he was, not what he does," the psychiatrist interrupted his speech.

"Oh, you ask who? Well," Sid stumbled, "I'll have to sleep on that question before I answer you."

In a way this whole story had really begun when Brian McFee (made an orphan very early) had come almost stealthily, like a housebreaker, to stay in the house of the renderer's son, though he himself had actually a much bigger and newer house left him by his dead Grandpa. The two of them, Roy and Brian, had one thing in common, their love of horses, and it was Roy who had taught Brian to love them. Roy's father had hardly been cold in the grave when the heir to what was later found to be a fortune took down the sign

RENDERING, SCISSORS-GRINDING, CISTERN
CLEANING

and put up the new sign

STAR-LITE STABLES, HORSES FOR HIRE

"There will be no more rendering, Brian." Roy had kissed Brian impudently, and drew him close to him, as if he would pull him all the way into his ribcage and imprison him there forever.

The immediate way Roy had got "power" over Brian McFee had been through dope and sex. Brian had got a taste for the latter by going several times to New York City where he had slept in the trucks and docks off West Street, and unaware of any danger had been initiated into almost every experience known there to men who love men, and when he had come back to the "Mountain State" he had made a bee-line for Roy, who else? That is, who else was lost to society but the renderer's son, and as he came through the screen door unbidden he had flashed his schoolboy smile that had done such wonders for him in New York, and he saw at once that cold and hard as Roy was he was just the same a pu-shover for him, so that they had sat and talked a bit embar-rassedly at first, for they both knew what was coming, dis-cussing things like mountain weather, shoeing horses, the upkeep of their cars, until Brian, growing more and more fiercely fidgety, had blurted out:

"Roy, have you got any dope?"

Roy had clammed up, then changed the subject.

But Brian felt that he had to have some before he threw himself at Roy's feet, which is what he wanted to do; that is he wanted to go over to him body and soul (he had thought this out in one of the empty warehouses off West Street), for he felt he must have a "master" to direct and guide him, he could no longer go on alone as the heir to his dead Grandpa's fortune.

Roy meanwhile angered and even a bit scared by this proposition, for Brian, like the De Lakes boys and Gareth Vaisey, came from the right side of the tracks, was old, old American stock, though come down considerably in the world, whilst he, Roy, was looked down upon as perhaps even lower than a nigger or Indian; Roy Sturtevant then waited, bided his time or more truthfully just held his breath.

"What if I was to say I did have some," he finally began. "What would you give me in return?"

Roy had heard of his rich uncle in Key West, Florida, who sent him expensive clothes, gift certificates, and other presents and remembrances from time to time.

"Money, of course, Roy. I ain't exactly strapped you know."

"I don't need money." Roy curled his lip.

Brian had blushed then and Roy knew he was in love with him, in love with him bad.

"Supposin' I did have grass or maybe something stronger, and say I was to give you some, I bet you would go straight and blab it all around, you know you would."

This was taking place about a year after the High School Graduation Exercises at which Sidney De Lakes had slapped Roy Sturtevant in front of almost the entire graduating class. (Some say he spat in his direction also.)

Sometimes at this same period as he lay tossing and turning in his bed at night, Roy Sturtevant would cry out, "Mama, help me!" She had been dead for nearly fourteen years, for Roy was now getting on to nineteen. "You should never have left me, Mama." She had threatened to do so once when he was only five—that is, one day she warned him she might have to go to *the little house that was in the woods,* so that forever after when he came upon a deserted house he would right away try to buy it, and then when he was eight she had done just that, had died and deserted him, and had left him abandoned in *his* house in the woods, while she had gone to some paradise where he could never join her.

He loved Brian McFee at that moment, as he pleaded for dope, almost more than he had his Mother. For one thing they both had the same kind of tender soft fair beauty and the large luminous hazel eyes.

"I said, Brian," Roy stirred from his dream, "what will you give me was I to find you some stuff?"

"Whatever you ask, Roy. You know I'm not a cheap-skate."

"I hear an uncle of yours sends you nice clothes from Key West."

"Why, sort of nice, yeah . . . He's not really my uncle, though. He's a guy I met at a party once in Washington, D.C. Took a shine to me."

Roy pulled gently on his left ear lobe.

"I know you have nice underwear, Brian." His voice was barely audible.

"Who told you that?" Brian looked about him desperately, perhaps to see if they were alone.

"So it's true then. You do have nice underwear."

"How do you know if I do or don't."

" 'Cause I watched you take a crap once at my place here. When you let down your pants I seen you had expensive stuff on nobody around here ever laid eyes on let alone wore."

"Well, is that a crime to go well-clad?"

"Putting aside how you earned it, well, no, but maybe, say, I would want it in exchange for my stuff."

"Underwear, Roy, for stuff. You do surprise me."

"All right, be surprised some more and let me have it."

"You'd really take it in exchange?"

"For a lid, yes, sir, I would."

"O.K., when do you want it?"

"Now."

"Don't you want . . . clean underwear?"

"I want it now in exchange or the deal is off."

"But what are you going to do with it, Roy? I mean—"

"That's my business."

"All right." Brian stood up. "Where should I change?" He began looking around him uneasily.

"You can change right here and now before me."

Brian waited only a moment, then began taking off his clothing, but he was trembling something awful. He shook all over. Finally Roy stepped forward and helped him off with the last of his togs. Except he wore his shoes and socks still. He looked painful naked and on the point of almost turning blue.

But Roy was examining the underwear like a jeweler going through the works of a watch.

"Don't you ever bathe, Brian?" Roy spoke at last.

"Not often, and neither do you," the boy snapped back at him. "Now give me my stuff, why don't you."

"This underwear is pure silk and imported to boot. Paris, France, huh? Hand-stitched! What kind of a man give this to you?"

"Where's my stuff now, Roy?"

Roy looked him lazily up and down, making Brian blush furiously again.

"See that little bureau over there with the glass top to it. You'll find what you want in the first drawer, in the left-hand corner. Your lid is waiting there."

Brian hobbled over to the bureau. Being naked or ashamed made him walk almost like a cripple.

He opened the bureau drawer and touched the lid. Then he grinned.

"And in the third drawer you'll find some old but clean-laundered underwear of mine. We're about the same size. At least in some places."

Brian turned back to eye him wonderingly, then opened this other drawer and hastily put on the clean underwear that belonged to Roy.

Roy had sat down and was watching him put on his other clothes. Meanwhile he had rolled up Brian's soiled underwear and put it in a large blue shopping bag.

"Brian," he spoke more calmly now, "come over here."

"You had second thoughts about our bargain?" the purchaser replied worriedly. "Because if you do you can have more underwear from what I've got at home."

"I don't want no more underwear, and you know it . . . I want you."

"What does that mean?" Brian said, pouting and his face going all kinds of colors.

"Quit stalling and playing me for chickenshit, Brian. I know how you got this underwear. . . . Only I love you, do you hear. Do you?"

"I guess I do," Brian replied, looking away.

Roy jumped up and took hold of him and drew him toward him.

"Don't hurt me, Roy. Please."

"Why do you think I am going to hurt you?"

"I can't stand pain, Roy. Please."

"Come here, Brian. Sit down on my lap now and get quiet."

Brian sat there and suddenly burst into tears.

"I knew you would get power over me," Brian said after he

had let Roy kiss and hug him and put his hand in his bosom. "I knew this would happen."

"Quit blubbering, will you."

He had soon undressed Brian all over again but as before he was allowed to keep his shoes and socks on.

"I will even give you your expensive underwear back if you want it."

"No, no, you keep it, Roy. It's yours by our bargain."

Roy kneaded and then almost tore the young flesh that was now abandoned to him. (Brian was then just sixteen and a few days.) And this was the beginning in the boy's phraseology of "Roy's having power over him." The slavery was to sicken both of them, and it was too strong and consuming to last. But through Brian McFee, Roy was to get at "softening up" Sidney who had insulted him publicly and who had for so long "kept power over him" since the eighth grade.

Two shattering events therefore never left his mind or heart: his mother having gone to "the little house in the woods," abandoning him thus forever, and Sidney De Lakes slapping him at the High School Graduation Exercises, and these two events, which never stopped in time, kept being projected ceaselessly in his brain like a movie that goes on being shown in a theater throughout eternity, giving him no rest or respite or calm, no momentary quiet, even in sleep or when insensible with what he constantly smoked.

The night Sidney had slapped him at the High School Graduation Exercises, the scissors-grinder (as the boys nicknamed him) had come home very late, having sat at the edge of some farmer's cornfield until the moon rose, and then going into the hall bathroom, had taken the straight razor made in Germany which his Dad had later slashed his own throat with, and had carved out a place by his right eye where the middle finger of Sidney's hand had struck him, the wedge cut there quite deep so that he would never be able to forget the insult, and tonight as he let his face fall over Brian's unprotected sex, he put the scar of his self-inflicted wound directly over the boy's penis and let it bob there again and again, that was all he seemed to want just then from the terrified, even slightly delirious McFee.

Then after this peculiar pantomime Brian felt Roy's mouth take his penis not like a lover, not like anybody who had desired him before but like something not quite human. He suddenly lost his fear of what was happening now through a greater fear of his losing his will power and direction to a man who lived only in the memory of his shame and anger.

Then abandoning himself in spite of his terror to Roy's lovemaking, Brian choked and screamed in a sort of piteous pleasure resembling, Roy thought, some small forest animal caught in a trap.

"Don't forget you are mine," Roy had said after they were through, and accompanying him out to the unpaved road which shown white in the darkness. Brian half-raised his hand to the places on his face where this new lover had broken his skin with his teeth.

"You can count on me," Brian had replied, after a wait.

"And you won't never go back on me, never, never?"

Even more than Roy, Brian had no one to hold on to at that moment, and he saw that without Roy and his terrible love, and his obsessive hate for another man, what was there for him but to maybe stay in his own dead folks' thirty-room house and die of sheer rich boy's neglect and aloneness.

"I won't never," Brian said.

"But you don't sound like you meant it," Roy complained, taking him in his arms again.

"When I tell you you're all I have," Brian got out huskily, "I mean it. I ain't got a soul on earth but you, Roy, so be satisfied."

Then he was gone, leaving the older man partly convinced and as much in love with anybody as a damned person can be.

"But I don't feel hate toward Sidney," Brian had said a few days later after they had become "fast lovers."

"Yet you always tell me you love me, Brian."

"Yes, yes, that's so." Brian was then silent. He had explained these silences in a phrase which touched even the scissors-grinder: "I am searching my heart for an answer." He had kissed Brian passionately when he said this the first time.

"Search away," he had told him, "then know you are all mine."

Then the day came when Roy said to him: "Why can't my enemies be your enemies if you really love me."

"It's true I could never be friends with Sidney now," Brian explained his feelings, "now, that is, I am in the know how he slapped you and insulted and shamed you in public."

"I would hope you wouldn't be friends with such a man," Roy spoke in almost wailing outrage. "I mean, should you go over to the other side now, I don't know what would happen . . ."

"Roy, what are you talking about. I've told you again and again you are all I have in the world. You brought me out and showed me what I am, what I feel deep down in me. So of course your enemy is my enemy." His voice faltered as he pronounced these last words.

"Sure, Brian, I believe the first part of what you said all right. But would you do something 'all out' to prove you love me as much as you say you do? That's what I mean."

"But don't I prove it, Roy," he cried, worry and a fearful dread coming into his voice, "when I give you all the love I have? Ain't that proof enough?"

"No, there's deeds, Brian."

"That ain't a deed, my loving you?"

"I need more proof, Brian. But I can see you only love me for my loving. You just love me in bed."

"Not so at all, Roy." But he said this with very feeble conviction.

"Would you kill for me if it became necessary, say?"

"Oh, Roy . . . You think now what you're saying. Kill for love?"

"That's what I said."

Brian shook his head. He was near tears, and reached for Roy's hand to contradict what he had just heard, but the older man angrily repulsed him.

"You don't love me, Brian."

"I do, I do. I love only you . . . But I can't kill for you. I *cain't.*"

Roy stood up and began pacing up and down the room, his hands in his pocket jingling some loose nails purchased from the carpenter's shed, his mouth drawn down at the corners. Despite his somewhat unkempt, even filthy appearance, he grew somehow, at least in the eyes of young McFee, more handsome daily, resembling an illustration of the Leatherstocking, a dirty Leatherstocking, it is true, and a more savage one.

"Roy, you should not even think such a thing, let alone say it. Why, it makes the cold shivers go down my spine."

"What crud talk is this?" He turned his full fury on Brian. "Look at this mark by my eye, look at it. He done that. Who? Sidney De Lakes is who. He tormented me all my young life with his contempt, never recognizing me in public, sneering at me in class, when here I done all his homework for him, slaved for him to see he passed the eighth grade and even high school, and all he let me do . . . was occasionally, behind the gym buildings . . . occasionally . . ." Roy's eyes went glaucous, almost blind; indeed they looked like the eyes of some disinterred statue. "Occasionally he would let me have him, and then spit on me after it was over for my pains . . ."

Struck by a kind of suffering he had no key to, Brian attempted to embrace his lover, but the renderer pushed him away. The nails fell out of his hands all at once.

"There he is," he raged on, "sitting in his house all these years amountin' to nothin' on account of he was a football star, too dumb though to go to college unless I went along beside him and did the drudge for him, worthless as the foam on homebrew . . ."

Roy stooped down and picked up one of the nails he had dropped.

"But he works at the filling station," Brian put in, in an effort to deflect the cyclone of wrath moving in the direction now of himself.

"Call that work, do you, huh? Look at my hands if you want to see work. See them?" He thrust out one hand displaying his sinewy fingers covered with cuts and abrasions, blackened nails and stubby thumb, into the boy's face.

"Who would miss him if he was to be killed, Brian?" He took the boy all at once in his arms and kissed his forehead. "Tell me, who?"

"Now you stop it, do you hear!" Brian shook himself free from the scissors-grinder. "I won't hear you talk about murder, Roy. Or I will leave you."

Roy lunged at him and held his throat in a vise which made Brian's eyes roll desperately, his lips go a strange purple.

"The only way you will leave me is in a pine box. You hear?"

Without warning he stabbed Brian's arm with the loose nail he had been toying with. As the nail went into Brian's flesh, both men exchanged looks as if to question why this was happening, who indeed had commanded it to happen. Then drawing the nail out slowly, wonderingly, Roy allowed Brian to slip to the floor at his feet, where he suddenly struggled for breath, coughing desperately and making retching sounds as he gazed at his arm bleeding from the nail driven into it with such force and passion.

"You belong solely to me, Brian McFee. Hear me? You are solely mine."

"What do you want me to do then, short of cutting my own throat for you?" Brian kept staring at his torn expensive shirt and the blood coming from the nail wound.

Kneeling down then over Brian, Roy said in mocking whisper: "I want you to act like you're Sidney's boy. . . . As a starter, get it?"

"But he goes for girls."

"Does he? Do you know how many times I've had him in the woods, the cornfield, back of the gym. You ninny."

Slipping off Brian's shirt now and then kissing the wound made by the nail, Roy put his face close to Brian's and said: "You both used to hunt together . . . So you go hunting

77

together again, then you can let it happen. I mean let him have you."

"And when is this to be, Roy?" He was still weeping from having Roy injure him so cruelly.

"Just as soon as you get the lead out of your ass. Now. I want it now."

"Well, I guess 'tis the hunting season all right."

"Yeah, 'tis, since you been filling your belly with the venison and quail I caught for the last four weeks . . ."

"I guess as usual you are right, Roy."

Roy rose over him, and kicked him indifferently, playfully, but hard, and then turned his back on him.

"I'll do it for you, Roy . . . I'll go hunting with him, and all the rest if I can . . . I mean I'll do my best," he cried in the face of his friend's stony silence. "But I won't kill for you, is that clear?"

Wheeling about and facing him, Roy started to say something, then, the anger in his eyes changing to a kind of sneering contempt, he took Brian's mouth in his and kissed him assiduously.

"Roy, you do love me, don't you . . . I need your love so bad, you know that. I wish I was enough for you so we didn't have to think even about Sidney De Lakes." But at a motion of anger from Roy, Brian finished: "I'll do what you command, though, never you fear. . . . I wish you wouldn't of stabbed me though with the nail." He held the sore place with his finger. "That weren't needed or right. I can't stand pain, Roy. It weren't right."

There was no way to do anything else but obey him. Brian had felt for some time that he was slipping away into the tide of the sea until Roy had chosen him for his follower, and before being chosen his hold on life had been so feeble that often he had slept through the entire day. Then Roy had come and taken him, and as a result he had felt if not wholly wanted and loved, at least consumed by a heat so intense that had it been relinquished if only for a moment, the frost and sleep of his old life would have suffocated and chilled him to death.

Brian on the other hand had a friendly good feeling for Sidney De Lakes and could never hate him, he assured himself. At the same time he was positive that he would never be able to persuade Sidney to have sex with him, for he was certain he was interested only in girls . . . But if Roy pressed him too hard, he supposed he would lie and say Sidney and he had done it together.

And so just a few hours later after the "scene" with Roy, and the threats and the withheld affection, and the cuffs and blows and nail wound, Brian found himself at the Piedmont Filling Station.

Sid had brightened at the sight of Brian and broke into a full-wreathed smile.

"What do you mean, do I like to hunt?" Sidney had answered at once. *"Everybody knows I like to. Of course I will go hunting with you . . . And why didn't you ever ask me before? I was just wondering who to ask to go with me . . . And of course I would like to camp out."*

The ease with which De Lakes had accepted his proposal so unnerved Brian he went home and didn't move for twenty-four hours.

They were gone (Sidney and Brian) three days and nights. They would have been gone longer but Sidney dared not lose his job at the gas pump.

Then of course Brian was summoned by his "lord" as soon as he had got back from the hunting trip, but he didn't need to be summoned. The vassal himself would have come as soon as he had parted with Sid to "report in."

"Brian, you better bring good news now," Sturtevant had said at once and pointed to a newly varnished wooden chair for him to sit down on.

"I always have the feeling, Roy, that if I was to bring you the sun and the moon on little platters, you would grouse and complain and send them back. I cain't please you. No way."

Brian burst into tears. Roy watched him and picked his nose in his customary obscene manner looking at what he picked before he wiped it on the sole of his shoe. (He knew of course how fastidious little Brian really was despite his trying to ape his own rough ways, and how much he loathed this particular habit of his.)

"So why don't you just give me the facts . . . You can skip the details since you are so wrought up," Roy advised him.

"Well," he said, still sobbing, "the first night nothing happened . . ." His eyes moved backward and forward as if trying to recall all that had transpired between them. "I didn't wear any clothes though as much as possible although the cold was pretty bad. I showed him every way I could that I was an easy mark you see . . ."

"Which you usually ain't of course."

"I felt something was in the wind though right away even before I stripped for him . . . I felt, well . . ."

"Yeah," Roy's nudging tone betrayed more than eagerness to hear the facts without the details so that Brian stopped and stared ruefully at him.

"It happened when we went to get the water from the spring. At the risk of pneumonia, I walked down there stark naked. He come along too with his pitcher. I couldn't believe my good luck. Without sayin' a word he put his hand on my behind as I was still drawing up my water pitcher. I just turned around when I finished filling it, and said, 'If you want some, Sid, take it and don't let's waste no time. . . .' "

Brian was almost unsure what had happened for a moment as he was telling of his "luck" for Roy was at his throat choking him, but Brian this time had wrested loose and struck the renderer a heavy blow over the Adam's apple. It nearly killed Roy. He fell, and lay gasping for breath, kicking with his feet. The wind was knocked out of him.

Then when his breath came back to him and he had got over some of the worst of the pain and the surprise of retaliation on the part of his pupil, Roy spoke penitently: "You'll have to forgive me, Brian . . . After all I ordered you to do it."

"Your damned tootin' you did," Brian raised his voice in indignant rage, acting himself like the master now. "I get your drift, too, Sturtevant. I see it all now, you cheap four-flusher. . . . It's you is in love with this Sidney De Lakes, ain't it . . . It's you sendin' me to be *you* with *him*, ain't it? Come on! . . . Well, you can go and get fucked by him yourself . . . I'm through, do you hear, Roy Sturtevant. Play me for a asshole, will you, and then choke me for doin' your biddin'. I'm through, you hear. *Hate him?* Balls. You worship him. He's your whole life, you filthy son of a bitch sneak."

"So what," Roy turned his full wrath now on his mutinous lover. "I say so what . . . So I worship and love him, and have for years . . . I also want to kill him and be rid of him and I'll see it done yet with or without your help. Now clear out. Get out. Get! Get out of my life. I don't want no more of you or your kind . . ."

But Brian McFee could no more go out of Roy's life than Roy could let loose or renounce his nagging obsession with Sidney De Lakes.

Once, just before his Dad's suicide, the old man had found a huge notebook hidden in Roy's room, its contents devoted entirely to Sidney De Lakes: snapshots, large photos, even pen-and-ink drawings of the football hero from the time he was a small boy on to just prior to Sidney's arrest and conviction for manslaughter. Had old man Sturtevant lived he would have seen more photos, more pictures, and read more news stories.

It was Brian also who had found the identical notebook just a few days before the "command" hunting trip. And he had been indeed as chilled in looking through the scrapbook as if he had found out also Roy was guilty of murder.

"He already in his heart is guilty of it," Brian had muttered, going through the pages of snapshots and keepsakes hurriedly (Roy had gone down to the privy at the end of his property, for the toilet in the house was stopped up). He had hurried looking as fast as he could, but the scrapbook and his mementoes had a fascination which made him forget time. Then he had felt Roy's hands tear the book from out of his grasp. But for once Roy did not say anything, or punish him.

Brian had heard his dismissal but did nothing about it. He sat down on the kind of folding chair popular at camp meetings and funerals. He put his head in his hands for a moment, then making a motion as if he was throwing his hands away, he cried:

"You cain't order me out and you know it!"

"You mean you aim to stay after what has passed between us here today?" Roy spat out. But he still spoke a little huskily and cautiously too owing to the choking Brian had given him, and the surprise he had experienced in finding out that Brian McFee might be a "slave" but he was a scrappy one and dangerous to boot. One could only push him so far, and that limit had been reached today.

"After all, you belong to me, Brian," Roy rose and came to stand over him.

"Do I?" the boy said turning to his tormentor. "Well, then, Roy, here I am."

Brian threw himself then into his "master's" arms, and Roy held him with genuine feeling, kissing what he liked to call his "mahogany" hair and stroking his thick soft eyebrows.

"You sure have the goods on me, don't you?" Roy quipped.

"Now what do you mean by that?" Brian complained, separating himself anxiously from the scissors-grinder's embrace.

"I mean, to choose at random, them keepsakes of mine all about Sidney De Lakes."

"Oh, them. Well, don't everybody keep snapshots and old souvenirs like that?"

"Maybe of their families they do, but nobody ever kept so many souvenirs as you call them of one man until I come along. No, not in all of history was one man so toasted and remembered and honored by the one who is so despised by him. . . . That is why I aim to kill him."

"But don't, Roy. Don't. Let him live. Let's us clear out instead."

"Us clear out for that little no-account gas-pump attendant? What kind of a friend are you turning out to be, Brian McFee?"

"Oh drop it then. No use talkin' to you anyhow. . . . But why ain't I enough for you?" His voice soared and his brownish-golden eyes looked like prize marbles. "Why don't my love mean more to you, huh? Why don't you give up this De Lakes man? What's wrong with you?"

"How in hell would I know what's wrong with me at this late date! After all I was never brought up decent like you with your rich Grandpa and these uncles in Key West and all. . . . But I know what I feel, and I know I want to kill him for what I feel and what he has done to me."

As he spoke these last words his own voice soared high in the register, matching the swooning crescendo of Brian's just moments before, so that the two voices, one coming after the other, resembled singers in some seldom-played oratorio.

"Maybe, Roy, I could go and explain your feelings to him," Brian spoke cautiously. "Maybe even he would apologize for what he done to you on Graduation Night."

"It's too late for any of that I told you!" Roy turned away from him, hiding his eyes brimming with tears. "You just work on gettin' him in deep with you, hear? That's all I ask of you. It ain't much either."

"Roy, what do you mean now by that! . . . I don't want to get in deep with him. What would I get deep in with him about anyhow . . . We don't have nothin' really in common. Just lettin' him have me at the spring and later, that won't never lead to bein' deep with him . . ."

"But you are in deep with me, Brian."

"Yeah, I guess you can say that again all right." He shook his head.

"Well, then wind him around your little finger . . . That's all you got to do. Make him dependent on you."

"I just doubt he cares very much about me. He just likes to poke me. That's about the extent of it . . . He likes my buns, he told me." Brian turned beet-red on saying this.

"And you say he ain't in deep with you, you shifty-eyed

little bugger . . . You know better! Once he gets in deep with you like that, we've got him. . . ."

"Oh, Roy, why do we have to get into trouble . . . It scares me so."

Roy took Brian's head in his hands and held his mouth to him. He kissed him solemnly a little like religious people sometimes kiss a favorite plaster saint in church.

"Make him pay for what he's made me suffer, sweetheart. Be *me* for him like you said a while ago which made me so mad cause it was the truth. Be me for him, hear? Make him care for you, make him want you till he busts, then hurt him. Make him smart for what he done to me, kid."

Brian dissolved now under Roy's kisses and embraces. Roy was like a virtuoso violinist that night as a lover, and Brian was the right and only violin, made by care and by hand only for him, and to be played upon with such consummate skill only for this one night, for as Roy kissed him again and again on every part of his yielding body, he knew he would throw him away instantly for the sake of his hatred for Sidney. Roy loved Brian deliriously but he hated Sidney De Lakes more. As he had said, he did not know why he hated so much, but he knew he was controlled body and soul by this hatred, and by his thirst for making his foe pay. And Brian was the one who would find out how to exact payment.

"Vance must never know about us now," Sidney said one evening as Brian and he lay together on the big davenport in the den that had belonged to Brian's Grandpa.

They had just come back from a short hunting trip, but had killed nothing. Brian did not like to kill animals, and Sidney had no real interest in hunting. They both used the sport as an excuse to be outdoors and in one another's company. They would fire their guns from time to time mostly to give each other the feeling they really knew how to shoot.

"Yeah, I bet Vance wouldn't understand what we do together if we was to draw him pictures," Brian retorted. "All he likes to do is study and go to church."

Sidney scowled morosely as he took in this remark, and removed his hands out of Brian's grasp.

"Well, it would kill him I think if he found out I sleep with you," Sidney was emphatic. Then too low to be heard: "He don't actually even know I am into men . . ."

"So it's him I guess you respect, huh, is that it?" Brian rose and glared at the man he had just poured out so much affection on.

"It's got nothing to do with respect, Brian," Sidney colored. "But we must keep it a secret from him. That's why your house is so good." He stammered badly as he got this out. "That's why hunting is such a good dodge."

"Maybe your love is a dodge, too, then," Brian almost whined.

When there was no reply to this statement, he went on lamely: "You do love me, though, Sidney, don't you? Say you do."

Even as he said this (though he felt love for Sidney, even a lot) he felt cheap and bad even asking such a question because the one he owed all his allegiance to was Roy Sturtevant. In fact when he told Sidney he loved him, he was only mouthing, he feared, what Roy had asked him to say. . . . And so though he did love Sidney in some ways more than he did the scissors-grinder himself, he felt more and more shamed and guilty and badly confused. He felt as a matter of fact, like a thief, and that he was constantly stealing.

"I told you how happy I was with you," Sidney spoke after

a long pause during which he had thought over whether he loved Brian or not. . . . As a matter of fact he did not think he had ever loved anybody. The closest to it in a funny way was Vance, but that was because Vance was so perfect and their relationship while deep was so distant.

Sidney began kissing Brian earnestly (actually it was Brian who had taught him how to surrender to kisses, and Brian was the first man ever to kiss him passionately), but without warning the younger man suddenly tore away from him and leaped up, for the thought of how he had promised to betray Sidney struck him full in his conscience at that moment.

"Brian, Brian, what's wrong now . . . ? Are you mad I didn't say I love you the most?"

"It's just as well I guess you didn't." The boy showed on his face all the anguish and pain he felt at that moment. "Fact is, Sid, I belong to somebody else . . . I am, to come down to it, somebody's 'slave.' "

Sidney put on his shorts and got up from the davenport. He was not sure now whether Brian had reference to the sex magazines he had been showing to him in which there were photos depicting older men having power over younger ones and beating them with chains and so forth, or whether he meant something even more sinister and real.

"What's come over you, Brian," Sidney wondered protectively. He took him in his arms, but that only made him tremble all the more violently.

"I've lied to you, Sid . . . I belong to Roy Sturtevant. . . ."

"Roy Sturtevant?"

He let loose of Brian as if he had touched a live wire. He wiped his mouth involuntarily.

"You mean to tell me you have been letting *him* make love

to you and then you come over here and mix the kisses you've had from him with mine . . . Why, you double-crossing little . . ."

But Sidney was too thunderstruck to finish the sentence, and could besides not think of anything bad enough to call Brian.

At the same time, looking at Brian who stood before him naked as a jay, he wanted him terribly all over again.

"There is no worse person in the whole wide world than the scissors-grinder," Sidney reported, looking down at the carpet.

"Why did you have to haul off and hit him at the Graduation Exercises that time?" Brian spoke accusingly.

"Oh, that." Sidney thought back. "He still remembers that, does he?. . . . Well, see here, he had badgered me all that evening, wanting me to autograph his Annual, wanting this and that . . . Wouldn't let me alone. . . . Matter of fact he has been pursuing me back as far as I can recall . . . Used to stare at me in the eighth grade like he seen Jesus. . . . Later on, always followed me into the shower after gym class . . . I knowed he had it bad for me, and I hated him for it . . . And once, well . . ." Sidney suddenly spoke like one who talks in his sleep, and Brian felt he had all at once forgotten he was even present, for Sid's eyes moved out toward the direction of the corn field. *"Once, then,"* he went on, *"it was after gym class, everybody had left the shower room but him and me. . . . In the shower he looked sort of handsome, certainly strong because he had been climbing ropes and doing the horse and the rings . . . Anyhow, he stepped over to me and says right out, 'Let me have you, Sid, right here. 'Twill only take a minute, and you'll like it.' I don't know what come over me, I let him suck me . . . I thought he would pull my guts and soul out of me he pulled so hard. I felt my cock had been swallowed by a shark. The pain and*

pleasure, confound him, was too much. . . . Then when he had finished me,
I pushed him down on the floor and kicked him, and run out of the shower
without my towel wrapped about me, stark mother bare-assed into the hall
where the teachers and students were milling about. . . . I was that
non-composed, you might say . . ."

Then turning to Brian and keeping his eyes fiercely on
Brian's eyes, he concluded:

"But I never meant to hit him the night of the Graduation
Exercises. I swear. I was proud too he was valedictorian. I
don't know what come over me. He wouldn't keep his eyes
off me that night either . . . I felt a funny fear . . . I felt
eventually he was coming to . . . take me over, take . . . all
of me . . ."

"Well, for your information," Brian spoke somehow with
indignation now, "he is my lover."

"And that turns my stomach, Brian. . . . I think you and me
are quits if you are sleeping with him too. I tell you, it's
enough to make me want to puke!"

Brian began to put on his clothes. Sidney paced the room
with growing agitation. He did not want Brian to leave him,
and yet . . . What was it with him, he wondered . . . Brian was
the only man he had ever really been close with, and in this
God-forsaken part of the world he could not hope to find
anybody to take his place.

But the thought of the scissors-grinder as his rival!

"Goodbye, Sid."

"Brian," Sidney spoke without conviction but with a certain sleepy stubbornness, "you wait now . . ."

"Goodbye I said . . . I mean it."

"Brian," he called to the retreating boy who was deserting
him, he realized, ridiculously enough, in his own house,
"you'll come back to me one day, you see . . . You'll find out

about Roy Sturtevant sure enough . . . You'll see I'm right in time . . ."

"So, Brian, you made two bad mistakes. What of it?"

Roy Sturtevant was too calm and collected for Brian McFee's comfort. He had expected Roy to fly into a passion when he told he had "broken" with Sidney and, what was worse, had let slip their secret that Roy was actually Brian's lover.

But instead of screaming at him or beating him or, as he had one day when he had been particularly angry with him, holding his head in the toilet bowl and keep flushing the toilet, today all he did was stand like a sentry before an army outpost with his arms folded and his face again like Leatherstocking, a brown, motionless mask.

"I would undo it if I could, Roy," Brian spoke, beginning to quail under this glacial calm.

"What do you mean if you can . . . You know and I know you can, and what's more you're *gonna* . . ."

"Now, Roy," Brian relaxed a little, hoping real anger would come for it would be better than this weird quiet and reasonableness.

"I'll tell you what to do," Roy began, letting his arms fall to his sides and then turning his back on Brian. "You use some pretext to see him. Go to the gas pump, or even write him a letter. Did you get far enough in school to write a letter so as one can read it? Whatever method you use, tell him you have broken with me. Tell him you are only his, nobody else's, and what's more, you was always his . . ." Turning around now he finished: "You can always meet me on the sly."

Unbeknownst to either of them, the cords were tightening

around both Brian and Sidney from that day.

The idea of writing letters to Sidney appealed to McFee somehow, despite his poor penmanship and his absence of ideas or power of expression, for he realized now that he cared deeply only for Sid, more than he ever could for the scissors-grinder, and so the daily letters to his love began.

Sidney was frightened nearly to hysteria when the letters began to arrive. He could not bear to see his secret life put down in black and white, as if pictures of him naked were circulating through the mail or posted on billboards. And once Vance had nearly opened one of the Brian letters by mistake.

Brian's letters were delirious, rhapsodic, idiotic, and im-plicating. Sidney burned them at once, swallowing hard as he held the match to them over the toilet bowl as if he was the flame that was swallowing them. He saved one letter, nonetheless, a very short one which he kept from then on in his graduation-present billfold. It read:

Take me back, and forgive me, or I won't last the winter. You know I love only you. You know I was meant for you from the beginning and I will always be yours.

This letter was not signed, and was written on a piece of Christmas wrapping paper.

The night Brian McFee was shot to death the sheriff ex-tricated another unsent letter, though already stamped, from Brian's breast pocket, which fortunately for his slayer was not yet addressed to Sidney and did not have his name in the salutation of the letter proper.

This "discovered" letter had puzzled the sheriff enough for him to go to Dr. Ulric, and show it to him in the hopes, according to the pained reluctant words of the officer, "It might throw light on the motive." The letter read:

There will come the day when you will see I loved you best, and though I was maybe sent to betray you and was in the hire, in your terrible words, of your life-long enemy, you should know in your heart that my feelings for you were the strongest. I have never wrote such a letter before, and I have the funny feeling somehow I won't never write another like it again maybe to anybody. If you will reconsider your decision I will do all in my power to change myself and make myself worthy of you. My idea of heaven is to be hunting with you in some beautiful park with mountains like here at home but where we won't need guns or prey but we will just walk together arm in arm in this good world and be by ourselves always together forever and a day. Brian.

The sheriff had studied Dr. Ulric's face as he read the letter, but the officer learned nothing from the old man's countenance; not a muscle moved during his perusal except for the steady blinking of his eyes, which was one of his constant and characteristic mannerisms for as far back as anybody could remember.

"So you don't have any idea a-tall as to who wrote this, Doc?"

"Couldn't even begin to guess," the Doc had replied, handing back the thin stained and now torn sheet of writing paper.

"It's a right odd letter, if you ask me," the sheriff persisted.

Dr. Ulric looked out toward the cornfield and the late afternoon sun.

That letter had been read at Sidney's trial of course, not once, but maybe three or four times, in an attempt on the part of the prosecution to make Sidney confess as to what it meant. But the defendant was steadfast in denying any knowledge of its meaning. It was only when he was back in his cell that he collapsed and fell unconscious to the hard cement of the floor. He was revived by a bucket of cold water, and then given a sleeping powder.

While the sheriff had been questioning the Doctor about the letter, getting nowhere with him, and knowing he was getting nowhere, he had suddenly nonetheless got a rise out of him from another quarter, and whereas he had encountered only the Doc's usual poker face and stony silence when discussing the "terrible" epistle from the hand of a young man already dead and buried, when the officer had said quite innocently, "Do you perchance remember the Ruthanna Elder case, Doc?", the Doc had dropped his brown cigarette (and the sheriff had picked it up for him) and closed his eyelids tight.

"Like yesterday," Charles Ulric had replied.

"This case reminds me of it somehow . . . Doesn't it you?"

"Oh, no," the Doc almost gasped. "That was a story out of my time and day . . . Yours, too, Johnson . . ."

"I wish you could remember this handwritin' as well," the officer said rising. . . .

"Ruthanna Elder!" the Doctor exclaimed to himself, and then aloud as soon as the sheriff had left. After having made the Doc lie about Brian's letter, the officer had given him back, perhaps as a reward, the memory of a story of "his own day."

"Ruthanna Elder!" he repeated time and again.

Toward the end of her life (she had died only last year, aged 60), she was called the "Sleepy-Time Gal" because she looked younger to the end than people half her age, and did nothing but sit summer and winter on the front porch of her house. Thinking, some people said. Ruthanna Elder who had been the high school graduation queen of a long-ago year!

That night, after the sheriff's visit, sleepless, Charles Ulric mixed and blended in his mind the story of Ruthanna Elder with that of Brian McFee and Sidney De Lakes, irrelevantly, perhaps, but inextricably, yes. He recalled that long-ago afternoon just before the graduation ball when Ruthanna had cautiously entered his office where so many babies had been delivered, where he had removed bullets from wounded men, had bandaged cuts and wounds, where he had pronounced men dead.

"No, you are not pregnant, Ruthanna," the doctor heard his own voice speak again in somber tones. "But why don't you marry your young man, Jesse Ference, in any case, if you're so worried, my dear . . . Get married, my dear . . ."

Ruthanna had cried then a lot, but had finally forced out: "It was not Jesse, Doctor . . . That is why I am worried. . . ."

"Did you want to tell me then who it was?" the Doctor had finally inquired after she had wept so hard and refused to get up and depart.

"It was my uncle, Dr. Ulric . . . That is why I worry so perhaps. . . . You see he approached me after he had invited me to his room to get a good view of the river and see where it had broken down the old bridge the spring before when it was at its crest. There was this fine view from the parapet of his Dad's house he claimed, and his Dad was gone . . ."

She stopped.

"Go on, Ruthanna, this is in confidence . . ."

Unlike most uncles, the Doctor recalled his own musing that afternoon, this uncle was two years younger than she, making him sixteen.

94

The uncle had closed and then locked the door leading to the parapet.

"But don't you see," Dr. Ulric had interrupted her story again, "You are not going to have a baby, Ruthanna . . . My examination has proved that . . . You did not conceive from your uncle's being with you . . . You'll be fine now for Jesse Ference. . . ."

"But why, then, doctor, can't I give Jesse my promise to be his wife? When it is after all Jesse that I love. . . . But no, the words stick in my throat . . ."

"But have you really tried to tell Jesse you love him and wish to be his?"

"Oh yes, of course, we have been sweethearts since childhood you know. . . . But as I say . . . I keep back the final words of promise . . . It is as though my uncle held my tongue. . . ."

"That is wrong," Dr. Ulric had almost scolded. "You must tell Jesse you are free now. And you need not give away what happened with a blood relation . . . Tell Jesse yes, that's all. Or tell him no . . . But you must not vacillate. . . ."

At the graduation ball, Jesse's face had blurred as she felt him hold her, and she could only see the uncle closing and then locking the door even as she was held close now to her fiancé's breast. . . . Yes, much as she loved Jesse, with all her heart, she could think of nothing but the closed door. Her uncle had removed her blouse and placed his young lips on her untouched breasts. She had melted under his arms like a river freed from ice.

Jesse had looked hurt as he had danced with her that night. He had looked like a man who has been slapped with a wet towel. He had always feared there might be someone else, but now, tonight, he was sure . . .

But there was nobody else of course, her uncle was not Ruthanna's love, her uncle had only taken her, he was not a real uncle after all but a boy, almost a child, but still, out of all the boys who had wanted her, had waited for her, he was the winner, and it was he who had first possessed her.

Jesse had walked away from the dance like a man in a dream, to the young uncle's house, the music drifting away now in the distance. A chance word from somebody had fanned his suspicions into flame. He had waked the boy after midnight. Jesse had asked him if it was true he loved Ruthanna. The young man had not denied anything; he had added all the missing details. It was the details that had done it all, people later said. Had the uncle only told the fiancé "yes" and said no more, what had happened would never have happened. But the uncle told it all so lovingly as if he were confiding to a kind brother, a brother whom he loved as much as he loved Ruthanna. He held Jesse's hand in his as he talked, he wept and admitted everything, he touched his face to Jesse's cheeks, perhaps he even added details which were not precisely consonant with the truth in order to please his visitor.

Jesse had stumbled out of the house at about daybreak. He had walked down to the Five Creeks, past the glue factory which had belonged to the renderer, then he went back ever so slowly to his own house and got the gun.

Ruthanna had been promised to Jesse since he was a boy. It was arranged you see, their marriage, from the "beginning," from, it seemed to Jesse, before their birth.

The young uncle was seated at breakfast, his eyes riveted on the comic section of the Sunday paper.

96

Jesse had walked up to him with a strange smile ruffling his mouth.

The uncle looked up, turned his untroubled gaze and brow toward his assassin-to-be. He had no chance to beg for pardon. Jesse shot once, then twice, the bowl of morning cereal was covered with red like a dish of crushed berries.

Jesse walked out with comely carriage to Ruthanna's house. He stood before the white pillars and fired the same gun into his head, his brains and skull rushed from under his fair curly hair onto the glass behind the pillars, onto the screen door, the blood flew like a gentle summer shower. Jesse Ference lay on the front steps, the veins in his outstretched hands swollen as if they still carried blood to his heart.

Then to go back to Gareth's accident. Gareth of course was driving, but how was he driving?

After Brian McFee had lost Sidney's love, he sought out the only other possible person who might go hunting with him. (Roy during this time was cold as ice to him, he had failed him, he was through with him, he would never speak to him again, he might even murder him . . . The only way he could take him back was if he "killed Vance's brother," and that was that, etc.)

Brian had a little more trouble leading Gareth "astray" than he had Sidney. But not a whole lot more. The trouble actually came after he had got him. Gareth almost immediately grew overfond of grass, and wanted more and more of it. The price for so much grass was Gareth's (in the words of the court which convicted Sidney a few weeks later), "moral obloquy," for the court had insisted the letter found in Brian's blood-soaked breast pocket be read again at the conclusion of the trial, and the prosecutor had said right out that the letter showed that it was addressed to Sidney and that the two men, McFee and De Lakes, had some deep and unwholesome friendship.

That was really what had convicted Sidney De Lakes. The accusation had sent Vance home with a sick headache.

The "moral obloquy" of Gareth Vaisey was completed in less than a month, and the death of his father and two brothers and his own physical and mental ruin came just a few days before Sidney shot and killed Brian.

For on the day his unsuspecting father and his two brothers elected Gareth to drive them and a trailer with the new horse just purchased in a famous stable in Kentucky, they had no idea they were going to their death because of the fact Gareth had elected to choose a "life style" (a phrase used in the trial) as utterly unknown to them as Sidney's romance with Brian McFee was utterly unsuspected by his brother. For in the words of the scissors-grinder, Roy Sturtevant, Brian had merely let Gareth find out who he was, anyhow, that is, the only thing he really liked was to have Brian McFee lie naked on him all night long and he liked even better smoking grass —six, eight joints a day if possible.

Gareth had seen the fast train coming that evening, but it was not real to him, it was only lights and sounds, red and yellow and harmless in the thick dark of evening coming to meet night. And then Brian had appeared on his horse! Or seemed to appear! "Race me, Garey, you race me now . . . Beat me if you can to the crossing, double-dare you!"

"For God's sake, Gareth, back up or go forward fast!" his father had cried and his hands were reaching out from the back seat to grab the wheel when there came the crash like world and sky had collapsed together in fire, and a stream of hot blood rained from everywhere, stinging the eyes and lips.

A little less than a week later, in the Bent Ridge Tavern, Brian McFee had thrown down his gun after having tried to shoot Sidney several times in the nearby woods, and made no effort to protect himself when Sidney raised his own gun and deliberately aimed it at him.

"Don't shoot, Sidney, I love you . . ." Brian called to him.

It was the surprise of those words which made the gun go off twice in his shaking hands, Sidney had told his lawyer.

"And do you expect anybody to believe that, Sidney, even if I could persuade myself to."

"I'm telling you what happened, sir."

"And this anonymous letter, Sid, you said you received just before the shooting at the tavern." He consulted his notes. "The letter said, *'Brian McFee aims to kill you tomorrow!'* Isn't that right? Isn't that what you say the letter said?" The lawyer checked his notes again. "And furthermore you say you burned this self-same letter?"

Sidney only stared at his lawyer. A few bubbles of spit formed on his mouth.

"When I heard Brian say, *'Don't shoot, Sidney, I love you,'* you see I believed him . . . I knew he meant it. . . . I didn't ever mean to shoot him just then even though he had been shooting at me back in the woods, but I knew why he had shot at me. It was for the same reason, don't you see, he loved me."

The lawyer folded all his papers and put them in his briefcase.

"You get a good night's sleep now, Sidney," he advised, rising and taking his client's hand. "But what you just mentioned now, keep that all a secret like something that never happened, understand? He never said that to you so far as we are concerned. . . ."

The deposit of spit on Sidney's lip slipped down his chin

and onto his sleeveless sweater, onto the floor. He heard the attendant let the lawyer out and close the iron door.

Roy, his mission or errand completed at Mrs. Vaisey's, had come back to his own house fully expecting to find his "suppliant" waiting for him, but there wasn't hide nor hair of the "Murderer" as Roy called him to himself from time to time. He had slipped out the back window.

But Roy had a hunch where he might find him.

There were several times since his return from jail when Sidney would steal off by himself and go sit down on the front porch steps of Brian McFee's house. The red-winged blackbirds were making a fuss in the wet and swampy places and in the wild cherry trees that grew behind the old untenanted property. Sidney always marveled how so young a man as Brian, who was so childish in so many ways, could have lived alone like this after his Grandpa died, with only the red-winged blackbirds to keep him company, had fended for himself, and then once near the end of his brief life, Brian had said to him, "All these years, Sidney, I was waiting only for you."

The more he thought about his own life the more he considered himself now a killer; in jail he had felt, had known even, he was innocent, but having come back to the "Mountain State," he felt he was at fault. At any rate he had been the instrument of Brian's death. And he knew deep inside himself that one day despite his horror that Brian had been the lover of Roy Sturtevant and had therefore soiled himself, he knew that one day he would have asked for Brian to come back to him. As a matter of fact he was priming himself to ask Brian to come back just a day or so before he received the anonymous threat.

During and since jail Sid had got more and more to talk to himself. "I think my heart will break" was one sentence he kept mumbling aloud, in a dry, cold, expressionless voice, perhaps even without feeling anymore.

He knew that today it would not be good for him to "break in" and look around the house where he had been so often with Brian, but maybe it was the sound of the red-winged blackbirds that made him so starved for some glimpse of Brian again. So he broke open the door and went in.

They had done nothing with the house in all these years, it was abandoned and yet everything was in its place still—the kitchen stove (a good one), the huge cupboards, the linoleum (brand new in its day), in the front parlor a grandfather clock, mute, but even stopped the very embodiment still of Father Time, the immense dining room with twelve chairs grouped around the elegant mahogany table.

Sidney, as in his other past visits, had planned to go upstairs, but he began to have the funny feeling around his heart again, like he had the first day he had called on Gareth and Mrs. Vaisey, so he sat down in the parlor until the painful sensations should subside.

He felt he could almost smell Brian. Then without warning he began to sob and cry. He saw that his whole life was a failure and that he was nothing, and the only thing that had meant anything to him had been Brian and he had snuffed that hope out. Finally he made himself get up and go upstairs. There was the bed they had slept in, the moths had been into the big comforter that covered it, and there was a musty stale odor but mixed somehow with the aroma of lavender. He opened the window with great difficulty, and then sat down by the bed in a rocker.

Outside evening was falling, the birds were now still, a crescent moon was rising.

"Brian, Brian," Sidney called, and then feeling a presence, turned and saw the renderer.

"Brian can't help you no more, Sidney, if he ever could, but somebody else has been busy doin' you a favor today . . ."

"So you come here too," Sidney whispered.

"I have gone to the trouble of having you reinstated with Mrs. Vaisey," Roy said as he knelt beside Sidney seated in the rocking chair. "You hear?"

"How did you do that?" Sidney said, breathless as he felt Roy kiss him in, he supposed, mockery.

"I all but own the Vaisey house now," Roy said.

"You do?" Sidney said moonily.

"I have since before you got out of jail, matter of fact."

Sidney turned his face away from the scissors-grinder.

"So your post is waiting for you again, if you want it, hear? Gareth is waiting for you . . . They have both missed you a lot . . . You listening?"

The renderer suddenly shook Sidney with fury.

"I heard you," Sidney answered.

"Then you get on back over there, I say."

"I'll go by and by, but will you just let me sit here in peace awhile, mind . . . ? Huh?" He turned his full gaze on his tormentor.

"So he sent you back to me" was all Gareth said when Sidney arrived, having already been greeted as effusively by

Irene Vaisey as if he were the great specialist they were always talking about and whose coming would immediately cure her boy.

"I wish you wouldn't put it that way, Garey," Sidney replied. Gareth sat in the very same chair and wore the very same clothes as he had the day Sidney was dismissed from serving him. But his face was thinner and sadder, and his eyes flashed some poorly repressed fury and smoldering disappointment.

"He has us now where he wants us," Gareth said.

"You won't let me kiss you, Garey?"

"No."

"Suit yourself then . . . You don't love me anymore?"

"I'll tell you by and by."

"That means you don't."

"You shouldn't have come through him." Gareth returned to this.

"But I was drove out of your house by your Ma . . . What was I expected to do?"

"Knock her down and stay . . . Kill the bitch and rule instead of her."

"He has always been like a goblin or booger watching me," Sidney began without warning, talking about the scissors-grinder like he was alone at Vance's and his house and watching the thick wet snowflakes fall over the stunted cornstalks. *"You say I shouldn't ought to have come through him. Everything has come through him. From the beginning. I'm telling you,"* he sat on the floor now and took Gareth's indifferent hand in his. *"Once when the snow was beginning to fall for the first time that year—we was in the eighth grade together—and because the weather was bad we could not play outside in the recess yard. . . ."* Gareth closed his eyes and swallowed. *"Like I say with bad weather, Garey, we played and ran downstairs in*

the school basement where they had a big old track for running, as big as if you expected horses to gallop there. . . . For to tell the truth even then I felt he seen me as a horse as he watched me run from where he stood on a little balcony they had built over the track. He was gazing down on me. He looked older than me, and he was taller. I run faster and faster around the track and he never took his orbs off of me. Sometimes he nodded, and I would lift my eyes and follow his eyes as if he was the runner. . . . So when I shot Brian McFee that afternoon the first thing I thought was I was rid of him, *that is rid of the renderer, the scissors-grinder, you follow me? I felt they would hang me and I would be rid of him . . . But I believe if I was to die and am buried a hundred feet deep he will dig me up and render me . . . I do for a fact. . . . Sometimes I think the safest thing to do is maybe surrender to him. . . . Except I have you, don't I, Gareth? . . . Don't I?*

"Anyhow, to go back to how he watched me," Sidney resumed when Gareth made no response, but showed he was listening. *"My running over the little track and he always watching me, you know . . . Well this one day, it must have been late fall and the last of the bad thunder-and-lightning storms before winter takes over had kept us all indoors, and like always on bad days I was running like a horse or colt and he was standing on the balcony like he was timing me, scowling, with his eyes almost closed, and I was watching him almost more than he me, and suddenly I turned around without warning like I was going to run away from him this time, and I run and crashed square into another runner at full speed. I was knocked down unconscious. A black fellow some years older than me but who was in my class as a 'repeater' stooped down and picked me up and carried me into the toilet, and had me sit on one of the stools, keeping my head down so that I would regain consciousness, but he had nothing in his hands or pockets to staunch the considerable flow of blood coming from my mouth and nose until like out of nowhere this brown not overclean hand stretched out and put in the hands of the black youth who was tending me a fancy silk handkerchief of the kind sent over the border*

from Mexico with exotic scenes depicted on it, just as I was coming to, and
I seen the hand of the son of the renderer extending the cloth which had
the faintest whiff of perfume too, but the cloth itself you could tell had never
been used at all till when it was thrust into those black hands to soak up
and wipe from my face the thick clots of blood . . . ''

Sidney had opened his mouth wide now as if to scream or utter some fearful blasphemy, but then instead he fell into Gareth's arms just as he had, that afternoon long ago when he was knocked out, fallen into the arms of his black rescuer.

Then something happened which brought Gareth and Sidney closer together, almost as close as Brian McFee and Sidney had been. The cause of their closeness was a dream Sidney had.

The night of the dream, Sidney had for the first time slept in the same bed with Gareth, and it was not too long after Gareth had turned out the lights for sleeping that Sidney had cried out with such force he had wakened the entire house.

In the dream, he later told Gareth, he felt that he had finally captured the booger which had been staring at him since the eighth grade. He had put him in a crate filled with clean straw, although he seemed to be still alive—at any rate his eyes moved from time to time under the straw. Sidney used a horse and wagon to transport the booger. They were headed for the rendering sheds.

When they reached the sheds, Sidney carefully took the booger out of the straw. His eyes were closed now but they pulsated under the blue lids and his mouth moved in a smile. He took off all the booger's clothes, which were actually corn shucks and wire grass braided tightly together. He removed his shoes and his socks, which were made however of spun gold (he was not at all surprised at that). Then the terrible part began. He put him in the boiling tub of sizzling, burning, foaming lye-treated water, and boiled and cooked him stirring all the time with a wooden spoon eight feet long.

When the "rendering" was done he took out Roy Sturtevant and he was a beautiful beguiling bouncing young man except he had no mouth. But he would take care of that, and he painted in the mouth, he painted it with blood from the edges of the rendering tubs.

Roy Sturtevant stood there in all his glory before Sidney, and then Sidney bowed his head and bent his knees and fell before him and kissed his feet and said, "You are the one I have been waiting for all this while. You are my life." But when he looked up, expecting to see the handsomest man who ever drew breath standing before him (for this was what the booger had turned into after his bath in boiling water and lye), he saw only a freshly picked clean skeleton save for the mouth which was all blood and a few bits of half-consumed flesh. . . . That was when Sidney screamed as if his lungs had been pierced with a thousand tiny needles. Footsteps then sounded from all through the house, doors opened, and Irene Vaisey stood before him more dreamlike and filmy than his nightmare in her shimmering white nightgown over which she had thrown a sumptuous purple dressing gown held together with a shining clasp. She had insisted Sidney take a tablet with a tumbler of water for sleeping which had made him so drowsy he was unable to tell Gareth what he had dreamed until the next afternoon just as the winter light was failing.

When Sidney told Gareth his dream then the next day when they were both more rested and composed and more used to being in one another's company again, Gareth's only comment was, "Roy don't render anymore if he ever did. The rendering establishment has been closed since the days of his Grandpa."

Gareth felt that closed the chapter and certainly made the dream of no significance, made it even contemptible.

He's got me in the same corner he had Brian and me in. This thought was on the very edge of being uttered, instead Sidney pressed his lips against Gareth.

"I don't never want to see the son of a bitch again, though," Gareth fulminated. "But I don't fear him like you do."

"I believe he thinks I am a horse," Sidney muttered.

Gareth stared at him now. If he had believed in anything like insanity he would have felt Sidney was insane at that moment, but he had never thought about the subject or heard it discussed for more than five minutes in his life, and he was not interested enough in it to take its existence seriously.

"I wish you was a horse myself," Gareth had finally commented. "We would have real good times together then instead of sittin' around here in our nightclothes like old women in the county infirmary. God damn it, I wish I didn't remember everything so well! That damned train done something to me deep-down I can tell you. I doubt, damn me, I will ever get over it if we don't find us a smarter doctor than the ones we have doctored with so far.... That's why I wish you was a horse, Sid, instead of a man. You follow me? You would make a wonderful thoroughbred. Maybe you can't blame the old renderer as you call him from being soft on you now, can you?"

"Oh dry up, why don't you ... You didn't hear one word of my dream because all you think about is yourself. . . ."

"Don't take on like that, Sid, when you're just back such a short while. . . . I listened to your dream but you shouldn't ought to even remember dreams on account of they don't mean nothing. . . . I knew an old midwife once (folks called her a granny-woman) who told fortunes for us kids by putting four flies in milk and the ones that didn't drown right away had a prophecy in the way their wings moved. . . ."

"And what prophecy did she give you, I wonder?"

Gareth screwed his eyes up and Sid was sorry immediately he had asked the question for it put the boy in such a state.

"She said I would be king of the owls."

"Oh, Gareth, hell, talk about dreams having no meaning. . . . You can't remember her fortune right if that's what you come up with."

"I was to be *king of the owls.*" He spoke testily and his golden brown eyes darkened. "She said it, hear, and I remember it."

"Well, then, she was a fraud at fortunes."

"No," Gareth proceeded now in his old moony fashion, "I think she was right. I didn't understand her, but I feel she told the truth . . ."

Christmas it snowed deep. It always does this in the "Mountain State," roads become impassible, drivers and cars are marooned and sometimes freeze to death before they can be rescued. The wind screams through the pine and oak trees as if it could not wait to be rid of the Old Year.

Each Christmas Roy gave an elaborate celebration for Brian McFee just as he had when he was alive.

"Nothing is too good for you, Brian," he had said when they used to celebrate together Jesus' birth. "Nothing will ever be too good for you, nothing will ever cost enough, Brian," the renderer repeated the same words now that he belonged to the invisible kingdom.

"I know I will see you again," he said, kissing Brian's photograph.

One of Brian's secrets was that he loved toys right up until he died. He was a manly boy from his earliest years, riding horses, shooting like a marksman, hiking, enduring hunger and cold and pain, but he had kept all his dolls from early childhood where they were housed in a special room of their own. To this somewhat large collection Roy Sturtevant added each year a new doll. Brian's death did not stop his practice, and each Christmas eve he wrapped a new doll in elaborate yuletide wrapping paper, heavy gold twine, and stickers of reindeers and Santa Claus and elves.

This year, the last year he was to make a practice of this, Roy presented to Brian a $5,000 merry-go-round horse. He had not wrapped it, but had kept it hidden in the big closet that lay off his room. On Christmas eve he brought it into the room before the Christmas tree which he had trimmed himself (it had taken him over fourteen hours to get the tree properly trimmed, for Brian in all and everything was so hard to please).

When he set down the merry-go-round horse in front of the yule tree and the large tinted photograph of Brian taken at the age he took his first communion, he had half repressed a sob.

"Do you like the horse, Brian?" he had addressed the picture. "The eyes are made out of a right nice kind of glass, don't you think."

Then he began to bawl. It was the grass he blamed for his tendency to weep, or again he would blame it on the fact that each Christmas Brian receded a little farther away from him, the pain of losing him was a little less pronounced, and so he sobbed for that too perhaps.

"Brian, I have a confession to make," he went on, unwrapping a present which he pretended Brian had given him (a music box from Switzerland). "I am still in love with this little gas-pump attendant and former football star. . . . That I could be so smitten! . . . And by someone who has always treated me like shit . . . Won't I never be free of him . . . ?"

He sat there groaning, holding his knees. The tears had stopped flowing.

That was when he decided he would go peek in on the two boys he had brought together.

After all, unknown to everybody but him and Irene Vaisey, Roy now owned the very house the boys lived in. He was their landlord, though they were unaware of it. And what was to prevent him peeking in on them from the edge of the woods, for both the woods and the property were his.

"After all, I am on my own land," Roy said as he stood outside the Vaisey house in the driving snow. It was past midnight by now so Jesus had finally been born again, and as a matter of fact a few church bells down in the valley were ringing.

Inside the house, and listening to the same bells, Sidney tossed and sighed in that heavy, stertorous way only an athlete or maybe a dying person can, the breath coming from deep down as if the earth breathed for him. He got up and went to the toilet and began to urinate, careful to do it along the sides of the bowl so the noise would be less likely to waken Gareth. His urinating was vehement like his breathing, and as he held his cock in his one hand, steering it away from the water of the bowl, he was somehow reminded of a dray horse which as a child he had used to watch piss with such furious pressure upon the baked dirt road. As he was engaged thus, he lifted with his free hand the curtain of the little window directly beside him and looked out. He blinked his eyes. Could it be? It must be the snow playing tricks, or else his heart was acting up again. . . . But no, the scissors-grinder was down there looking up at his light. He did not even bother to put on his house slippers or his robe (actually Gareth's). It was, he felt, imperative to touch the specter this time. He would recover, he was convinced, if he touched him.

The figure of the scissors-grinder did not move as he heard the storm door open and the dry trudge of Sidney's naked feet in the snow as he approached him. When he advanced to within a few inches of Roy, Sidney heard his own voice say, "You can slap me now if that's what you've come to do, or if you want to shoot me, suit yourself . . ."

"I ain't made up my mind what to do. I'm lookin'."

"My face is exposed for you to do whichever thing you want. . . ."

"Barefooted, too," Roy said without half looking down at Sid's feet to pronounce on this. His eyes were focused on Sidney's mouth.

Almost before he had got the last word out, Sidney slipped and fell at Roy's feet. The snow was deeper than it looked so that he sank rather perceptibly in the drift he had landed in.

Roy did not move for quite a while. Then he slowly bent down, gazing fixedly at the gas-pump attendant. He nudged him with his foot. Sidney opened his eyes.

"I'm not ready for you yet," Roy told him, bending down over him.

He picked up some snow in his bare hands and rubbed it over the recumbent man's face, and then opening his pajamas a bit rubbed the snow over his chest and belly.

"My face is ready for you to do whichever . . ."

Then Sidney seemed to have passed out. Roy kicked him again with his hunting boots.

"Oh, well," he said after studying him for a while. The snow suddenly began to fall now in thick wet heavy sheets.

Roy picked up the unconscious man and threw him, unconcerned as if he had picked up a ten-pound bag of potatoes, over his shoulder. The storm door had been left open so that it was no trouble at all for him to walk right in, and then up the back stairs and into Gareth's room. Roy flung Sid down on the bed and Gareth woke up, if indeed he was asleep since he almost never slept, and he heard the thump and the words:

"Unless I miss my guess, I will be back for the both of you before too very long. . . ."

Later Roy Sturtevant was almost as unsure he had stood outside the football hero's window and then had seen his "principal" come down and out into the snow barefoot as Sidney himself had been unsure he had seen Roy and not a snowman, which he and Gareth had made the day before for their amusement and idle hours, and to have something like that to gaze down on as a kind of sentinel against their sleeplessness.

The sight of Sid's feet naked in the snow on Christmas had for a time mollified the scissors-grinder's hatred (yet only by dying could Sidney De Lakes make up for what Roy had suffered, only by hanging on some barren tree forever, ignored even by the fowls of the air and the beasts of the field who would find his flesh too rotten), but then, as Roy had sat in his drafty immense house, like an abandoned castle in the wastes, he went over, with the aid of a notebook he had kept since the eighth grade, all the slights and insults, rebuffs and insolence, the looking straight through him by the hero, as if he was air, the curled princely lip and sneer, the fine-chiseled nose in the air, the contempt and loathing and fury of all those years culminating in Sidney's striking him when the renderer had only reached the accomplishment of valedictorian by reason of his love for the football player. He had been slapped then, in other words, as his reward for an achievement which he had pursued and won only to impress the De Lakes.

He closed the notebook with a resounding bang, almost a crash like that of an entire forest of pine trees falling in a lonely stretch of timberland.

The De Lakes must die!

Nonetheless because he had felt such pleasure at having carried Sidney over his back that day and because he had felt such intense happiness at seeing those naked feet in the snow, Roy now stripped in front of a seven-and-a-half-foot mirror. He would punish in himself for once and all the pleasure he had taken by carrying the unconscious body of the De Lakes snot. His own body must be held to account for such weakness. His body must never yearn again for Sidney De Lakes. His body indeed was his enemy, along with the football star. And his enemy must die, but first to punish his body.

His father's German-manufactured straight razor lay nearby.

With a short-lived delirious kind of prayer, at least he closed his eyes and let certain words sizzle and boom from his white lips, then throwing his head back, with (to his regret) a sudden look of admiration at the way he had made his physique resemble that of a Roman statue by dint of incessant hard physical labor about his house and farm and pasture and woodland (it was his body after all which had made Brian

McFee dizzy with delight and which in the end had been the instrument of his death), he slashed then his wicked arms which had enjoyed the weight of the gas-pump attendant, and when these bled to his satisfaction he slashed his feet and their veins for having admired the naked feet of Sidney De Lakes, and then he slashed the flesh over his heart for, despite all his warnings to his heart, it had continued to love and adore his arch-enemy.

But he would not die! No, he must live as a real renderer and grandson of a renderer, with these new scars, with the fluent loss of new blood, he must live in order to fulfill his final revenge against the enemy who had dictated the whole tenor of his life.

The worst of winter was perhaps over. Roy had recovered from his wounds. He spent hours admiring the scars on his body, the pink cicatrices of his victory. As he grew older he looked more and more like an Indian. There was not an extra ounce of flesh on his spare sinewy body which resembled certain trees or vines so austere in their configuration that it is said even birds dare not alight on their branches and animals pause on confronting them and then make a wide detour around them.

He combed out his long black hair meticulously today, almost tearing from the roots any strand which snarled or refused to go through the fine-toothed yellowed ivory dressing comb. He put on a suit of clothes which he had purchased through the mail. (He hated the haberdashery store which was located a few steps from Doc Ulric's.)

He polished his shoes until they gleamed like silver pools in the forest. Then he put his fingers and hands in soapy water, and tried to manicure his nails which like wild creatures suddenly trapped and tamed by men remained no matter what was done to them indomitable and black.

In his ears, after sudsing and rinsing them incessantly, he daubed an expensive bay rum which he had bought also through a mail-order catalogue.

When he was perfect, he got in his car and drove to the door of Irene Vaisey's house.

At first she had sent word with her "butler" that she would not receive him.

"Tell her if she wants a roof over her sick brat's head tonight, to get down here."

"And," he shot at the retreating back of the servant, "tell her I don't have forever . . ."

She appeared almost instantly, trembling badly, at least in her hands, much thinner than he had ever remembered her, and despite her haggard cheeks and eyes, younger and even more beautiful. Her beauty infuriated him even more than it disgusted him.

"What more can you have to say to me? . . . I have reinstated him, I have followed your orders . . . Shall I go live in the county infirmary for you?"

"You will not address me in that fashion," he spoke so low, yet so loud.

"I beg your pardon," she whispered.

"You have no right to sue for or bestow pardon. Everybody knows your moral character, and that you are unfit to take care of Gareth. Whores like you have no right to see their sons after the moment the son has emerged from your stinking . . ."

"Get out of my house," she said, offering to hit him.

"You will sit down and listen to me, or Gareth and you will spend the night on the road."

Irene Vaisey raised her hand to slap him again, but she had no energy, no will. She sat down.

"Leave her alone, Roy."

It was Sidney who had just said this as he entered the room.

The renderer opened and shut his eyes several times. The Sidney that stood before him just then looked like three men, he looked like the snapshot he had taken of him when he was the idol of the high school, he looked like Brian McFee when Brian had bestowed all his love on him, and he looked like the yellow-gold-eyed Gareth. He was all the temptations of his life standing there in blinding glory.

"I'll surrender to you, Roy . . . You can have me . . . instead of . . . them."

He waved his arm in the direction of Irene.

"Just go, Roy, and I'll make up for everything . . . All the back payments."

Too astounded even to accept such an offer, too blinded again by the countenance of the man who in the end directed his every move, he took up his brand-new hat which had the price tag still sticking in the brim, and left the room, walked down the long tier of front steps, and they heard him drive off like the north wind.

"It ain't right you and Gareth should be involved," he began, unaware of her condition, unaware of her bewilderment and even horror, and certainly unaware how *he* and not the renderer had frightened her by this speech he had made, by his "surrender."

"I don't understand any of it, do I, Sidney?" she implored him.

He never looked at her as he began speaking, much in the way he had spoken in court and said, "I'm not sorry," which the judge and jury had thought meant "I am not sorry I killed him" when he had meant "I am not sorry I loved him. I am not ashamed I have been the lover of Brian McFee."

"He has been waiting for me all our lives, him, me, like two heavenly bodies in space that they have predicted will one day collide."

She cried a little, then stopped in order to listen more accurately.

"I have been running away from him since at least the eighth grade when I was fourteen, and he used to hand me the correct answers to my arithmetic test under the seat behind me. He used to hand me the right answers also on history and geography exams when he seen I was stumped. . . . All those years, though I pretended I never saw him, I guess though I saw only him and knowed he was always present. I felt when I was in jail he was in the next cell. So why should I spoil the rest of everybody's lives, so why not quit hiding lest I go shooting maybe somebody else, why not just go to him. . . . When I had this trouble with my heart in prison they thought for a while maybe I could use a pacemaker . . . Then they said no, I didn't need no pacemaker. And the reason they arrived at that decision is I think they realized already I had my own pacemaker, which is the renderer. For the pacemaker that they finally heard ticking in me is the scissors-grinder's heart, which beats for me. When he is happy, which ain't often, my heart beats better, but when he scowls and is mad, my heart is sluggish and beats thickly like now. . . . When he is quiet, I am at prayer. . . . I have been too proud, Irene, but my pride ain't no match for his. He has the pride of some king of a whole world of hemispheres, under the ground and the rivers maybe, but he is king. I see that now. He is stronger and bigger and smarter and both younger and older, he is taller and more cunning and runs faster despite all the years he just stood idle and watched me run for him, why, I bet he would outpoint me in football now and maybe would of way back then, and I have been running away from him when had I just thrown myself at his feet like he wanted me to do at the High School Graduation Exercises, I would have maybe been rid of him, yes, had I throwed my arms

around him in the eighth grade or marched with him to the urinal and let him do every whichever, with me, it might have been better, though I doubt it. Even when I surrender, if I do, and I know it is what I will have to do now, it won't be enough for him, or say I lay down my life for him and let him render me into fine perfumed soap for him to wash his hands with and maybe his rectum, it won't be enough. He will curse this soap for not being Jesus and his sunbeams. It won't be enough, for nothing will ever be enough for him, why, as I say, if Christ and the Angels was to come down to earth and renounce their power, and say, 'Scissors-grinder, use us meanly as you wish, destroy us and render us, and make us into tallow, and we will fall down on our knees and worship you,' he would do it. That is, he would render Jesus Christ and the Angels, but he would not be satisfied. If he was King of the Moon and the Sun and the mountains of the furthest away galaxy and appointed Emperor of all Space, it would not be enough for him. I know I am right. . . . Nonetheless, my offer to him holds good. I told him I would surrender, and I am tired of the waiting and the pretending, and thinking I see him everywhere, in snowmen, in dusty roads in autumn, in the sunflowers when they droop in the drought, in the moon when she is horned or with a halo, and in the setting sunbeams, since he is everywhere then and I am cursed with him and yes I guess he with me, why not go to him on foot now the snow has begun to clear from the mountain roads. . . . Yes, I will walk over to his place and say, 'Roy, I've come to give myself up . . . You can render me, you can cut off my offending parts which have hurt you so long, you can do as you please, but I can't stand no more dilly-dallying putting off and procrastination. . . . Is that clear? I am winded and bushed and beat . . .' ''

Looking up finally Sidney saw what he thought for a second was another woman who had stepped in to hear his speech, but it was, after all, only Irene, whose face was furrowed and shrunken and disfigured by the grief of his words. She looked seventy years old in that sun-moted light stretching down to them from the stained-glass windows and walnut banisters.

"Do you have any word for me, then, Irene?" he inquired.

"None, none," she sobbed then. "But I may later, dear boy."

She indicated she wished him to leave the room.

"You cain't go to the renderer, do you hear?"

It was the next day and Gareth was standing over Sidney who was pretending to be asleep still.

"I won't let you," Gareth went on. He took Sidney's rough, heavily veined hands in his.

"I might have known your Ma would give me away," Sidney replied, keeping his eyes closed. "That's the damned woman for you, spilling my secret to you . . ."

De Lakes pulled his hands away from Gareth's grasp.

It was the first time the young invalid had seen him really mad.

"Look, if you go to him," Gareth took his hands again, "I'll go with you. It'll be better together . . ."

"You cain't go with me, what's wrong with you! You should be ashamed of yourself for even thinking you could. I am going and I am going alone and have it out with him. I see it all clear now. I have been hiding from him all my life. Did Irene tell you that too? And he has been waiting for me all that while and I have been chicken . . . So I am going and alone. Damn your mother for talking to you. . . ."

"I'll go to him, never you mind. I'll see him," Gareth responded, raising his voice and throwing down Sidney's hands from his grasp as he might have thrown down a baseball bat after he had failed to hit a ball for all of an afternoon.

"I'm glad though to see you full of piss and vinegar," Sidney opened his eyes wide and smiling now. He pressed his nose quickly against the boy's long silk-smooth hair. "But I don't want to hear no more about you facing the music for me, do you hear. . . . No, no, this is my turn to be valedictorian . . ."

"What if he should kill you?"

"Well, then, that would mean it was my fate from the beginning to have him do that to me. Be done in by the scissors-grinder . . . I won't hide no more. I hid from him by killing Brian, hid by going to jail, hid from him in the eighth grade and was really hiding from him when I hit him at the Graduation Exercises. No more! Let him do his damnedest . . ."

Actually it was Gareth who went that same night. He rode one of the only remaining horses after the house got still. The horse acted like it knew how important Gareth's going was, for it failed to make its usual whinnying sound and didn't kick once or resist the saddle and bridle. It was like a horse made of fog and air.

It was the first long ride Gareth had taken since before the train wreck, and he arrived tired. Furthermore he had not put on heavy enough clothing so that he shivered badly as he rapped at the door. For a minute he feared the renderer was not at home.

But of course he was and opened the door, his mouth going slack when he got a look at who it was.

"What are you shivering and shakin' for?" Roy inquired. "It's spring."

"I come to talk." Gareth pushed his way in.

"I don't suppose a well-brought-up snot like you imbibes whiskey even after physical exposure, does he?" Roy studied him under the dim light of the kitchen ceiling.

"Mind your lip now," Gareth managed to get out with difficulty by reason of his trembling.

Roy took down a bottle of Weller bourbon and poured him a shot in a high tumbler and banged it down before him.

"No thanks," Gareth said. He sat down on a high stool. "I don't touch it."

"You're a guest in my house and you'll drink it." He held the brim of the glass to the boy's mouth.

"I come here to ask you a favor, Roy," Gareth spoke into the glass now as if it were Roy. "If not for my sake, for Brian McFee's."

"Brian McFee don't need no intervention from you for him . . . I'll take care of that, and don't you never mention his name in front of me again unless I give you express permission for it. . . . Now drink this or I will smash glass and booze down your craw."

He poured the liquor down Gareth's throat.

"Take that fucking swill away from my mouth, do you hear?"

Roy threw the rest of the liquor in the boy's face.

"Suck the rest of it off of your mouth," Roy jibed. "Or shall I kiss it off of you?"

Gareth swallowed, trying to keep his anger down, and wanting after all to plead with the renderer for Sidney, for himself, for the house.

"Don't hound us, Roy . . . Give us a chance." He wiped his face dry with a handkerchief.

"Us. Mmm . . . Say you act pretty spry for a boy who is sick all the time . . . Horseback riding at two A.M. What is your ailment exactly do you say? According to the latest medical bulletin, that is."

"Far out, ain't you . . . ?" Then conquering his ire, he went on: "I come here unbidden and am not put up to it by anybody, Roy. . . . But you got to let Sidney De Lakes off of the hook! You hear? Let him go!"

"Huh, let him off the hook! . . . What about the hook up my ass . . . ? Did you landed gentry ever think of that hook?" Rolling his eyes, his mouth suddenly as wet as if he had drunk all the bourbon, he continued: "I'll let him off of nothing. . . . Let him die . . ."

"That's what I come to ask of you," Gareth spoke unlike himself, and his voice rose and fell as if he were singing a solo.

"Don't hurt him if he comes here," Gareth began then to plead in earnest. "But why don't you give us up. Whatever harm we done you long ago or you think we done, let up on us."

"Is that the end of your speech?"

"I can't tell it in words, Roy," Gareth almost whimpered, his strength and bravado diminished to nothing. "But I would do anything if you would let him go, once and for all." He looked up at Roy.

"I don't have hold of him. He has hold of me."

Gareth let his hands fall to his lap as if he had heard the judge pronounce the sentence. Quickly jumping up then, his face white as the recent snow outside, he pulled out a revolver and pointed it at Roy.

"You think I'm scared of that, do you, you chicken-shit little coward . . . Go ahead and shoot."

"You're going to promise me to let up on Sidney."

"So it all worked out the way I thought it would," Roy sneered. "And who reinstated him with you? . . . Did you ever think that out? . . . You must never have taken a good look at the son of a bitch, though, to be in love with him. For if ever you looked at him hard you'd see there's nothing left of him to love . . . Why, he's sicker even than you . . ."

"I prize him and I need him and you shan't get him from me or I will blow your brains out."

Roy turned his back on the boy.

"Go ahead, shoot," he would say every so often. This went on until Roy was prepared and ready and then wheeling about like some sparrow hawk from the sky, he swooped upon his assailant and tore the weapon from the boy's hands, hurried over to a commode and locked it in one of the drawers.

"Now command me, why don't you?" He rapped Gareth across the mouth with his knuckles. "You're like him, though, too incompetent to shoot when you had the chance. Did your old woman send you to kill me?"

"You'll regret this, Roy . . . If you don't let us off the hook, especially him." Gareth moved to within an inch now of the renderer's face. "What did he ever do to you that you hate him so?"

"You got gall to even breathe that question. . . . You never heard then he killed Brian McFee. And if you ain't heard he killed him, you don't know before he killed Brian he killed me . . . All those years through grade school and high school he was the one I thought about night and day. . . ."

Gareth backed away now in terror for as Roy spoke these last words he realized that the man speaking them was no longer aware of his presence.

"All those lonely years with my brute of a father, he was the one night and day who was in my thoughts . . . The first time I played with my own cock it was while I looked at a snapshot of *him*. . . . He owes me his blood . . . Go tell him he owes me his blood," he came out of his reverie now enough to glance at Gareth.

As he looked at the boy, one wild expression was followed by another, if possible, even wilder, at least a different cast of wildness.

Rushing to the commode, he nearly broke that article of furniture to pieces as he wrenched the drawer loose and pulled out Gareth's gun, and pointed it at his breast.

"Do you know where we are going to take the problem?" Roy inquired. "I thought you wouldn't. . . . Well, you went and mentioned Brian McFee's name, didn't you, though I forbid anybody to name him before me. . . . Well, we are going to Sycamore Lane Cemetery and pay him a visit, and ask him his opinion if I should let your lover off the hook . . . We'll go on your horse since you are so fond of traveling horseback . . . Now you march," he spat out, pointing the gun at his head and pushing the boy out into the night.

They rode together at breakneck speed on Gareth's horse, Roy taking the reins, Gareth holding on with might and main, as the renderer purposely (he felt) chose the worst and muddiest back roads, the loneliest, and of course the most unfrequented. It was beginning to drizzle a thin wet snow, though the crescent moon was faintly visible on a piece of the unveiled part of the sky.

After what seemed to a stricken Gareth an all-night ride, they came to the fence which surrounded the south end of the Sycamore Lane Cemetery. Roy studied the height of the fence, armed at its top with heavy iron spikes. Then lashing the horse with the riding crop, and letting out a cry that if any cry could would waken the dead, he cleared the fence with the horse in one mammoth straining of muscle and nerve.

Then Gareth heard the horse's hooves on fine gravel (he had closed his eyes almost from the start of the ride), and finally Roy's "Whoa!" pronounced in maniacal imperiousness.

In the silence that followed this daring and this outcry one heard the incessant dripping of the snowy rain from the pine trees.

Brian's grave lay before them, among many other graves which dated as far back as the Revolution, with a sprinkling of Civil War graves, and then all those other graves in honor of men who had fought and died for a cause. Brian had been allowed to be buried here because both his father and grandfather had fought for their country.

Without warning, Gareth pushed Roy aside, almost knocking him off balance, and taking off his hat, he knelt on the simple tombstone over which a small white angel rose in the act of reading from a tablet.

Gareth began intoning, holding his big wet broad-brimmed hat over his heart: "As you was the unknowing cause of the ruin of my family, Brian, and as you hear me on the other side, no matter where you are, I beseech you" (here his sobs from anger and confusion broke through his words) "beseech and entreat you, *Save my house from ruin, Brian, and mete out punishment to this hell-hound who is dragging us into the grave with you. If necessary let us die, Sidney and me and my Mother, but not by the hands of the aforementioned hell-hound. Brian, goodnight, and Amen.*"

But when he rose he looked into the eyes of the scissors-grinder, which by reason of the words he had just heard had made his features unrecognizable for a moment so that Brian let out a gasp of pure terror which was immediately stifled by Roy's hand clapped over his mouth.

"We will see if Brian McFee hears you now," Roy began, and he raised the riding crop and struck the boy across the mouth. Then throwing him to the side of the grave he pushed him flat on his face and with his knees in his spine tore off his trousers. He rabbit-punched him methodically, drowsily, and slapped the back of his neck until Gareth went into convulsions, then lay quiet, like a small prey the hunter has finished off by striking against an iron post. Loosening his own clothing only sufficiently to bring out his stiffened penis, leaving his balls draped and hidden as on ruined or defaced statues, and ejecting on his prostrate enemy's backside a profuse rain of spittle he entered exultant his disobedient pupil's body with authoritative but for him not vicious strokes. Then after a vehement endless time, as he was reaching climax he cried to the dark vault of the sky and also to the querulous statue angel standing guard over the grave, "Do you hear your one-time lover's prayer now, Brian McFee, in the hottest center of hell, do you? If so, send him a lightning shaft from wherever you are to show him the dead can do nothing about the living and cannot even tell earth from hell. . . . Do you hear, Brian, do you hear him bawling?" Here he struck the prostrate youth a rain of blows from the crop.

Pulling off all his remaining clothes, Roy then yanked the body of Gareth up, opened his eyes with his fingers, slapped him vigorously, spitting into his eyes and roaring a hurricane of insults into his astounded countenance, he put him on his horse.

"We'll send your ass home in real style now for your bedfellow and your doting Ma," Roy said as he tied him with cord and heavy rope against his falling off on the road home, and then pulling open a seldom used iron-gate he gave him a final sendoff with words so obscene and murderously loud Gareth thought his eardrums had burst, before whipping the flanks of the horse to make him run, the scissors-grinder screamed: "Ride home if you and that spavined brute have the know-how to and show your mate Sidney what's in store for him if he ever comes near to my land or property again. . . ."

Gareth reached home just after the first saffron streaks of dawn were visible above the mountains. The cord which had held him to his horse had come undone almost right away. He had met a few trucks on the way back. The drivers had stared briefly and one truck stopped, but then drove on. The man who brought the hay for the horses was standing in front of Irene Vaisey's mortgaged property when the horseman arrived, and he immediately turned and called Sidney who had just risen. Sid took one look and ran three steps at a time all the way upstairs for a blanket and house slippers. Then having wrapped Gareth to the eyes in the blanket, Sid let the boy walk upstairs under his own power.

"Yes, it was him," Gareth replied to Sidney's silent question at last. They both avoided looking at one another at that moment.

"If you feel you want to tell me what happened, go ahead," Sidney was saying, looking away from the torment and the sound of the boy's chattering teeth.

Gareth grinned, blurted out the worst and then lay down on the bed. He acted, Sidney thought with mild disgust, sort of pleased with himself.

Sidney had barely given Irene more than ten words of the story when she called the sheriff, but then, shamed and fearful of what the scissors-grinder had done and what more he might do, on Sidney's advice, she had called the sheriff back and told him not to bother.

"We won't need no sheriff," Sidney had told her. "I should have gone sooner to see him and this might not have happened . . . I will go now. . . ."

Instead he made a stumbling movement and sat down forcibly in a chair.

Despite what he had gone through, Gareth actually looked better and spoke more coherently and fluently than he had for some months. He was given a bath and some brandy and milk and put to bed, but he sent word down to Sidney to come up and talk.

Irene was standing, her arms folded, her makeup carelessly applied, her hair in strings. "You can surely tell your own mother," she was shouting to Gareth.

Gareth stared at her stonily. "One's own mother," he mimicked her saucily. "You can tell nothing to your own mother," he scoffed.

Then Sidney took over, and at a look from him Irene withdrew.

They began going over what happened, almost like lawyers discussing a badly written will.

"You already told me fifty times he tied you to the horse, Garey . . . But before that what?"

Gareth looked calmly at Sidney, his wild look of the past weeks, even years, was gone, never to come again. He would be collected and severe now until the end.

But without losing his quiet manner, he now raised his voice so that the whole house could hear him: "He did me in the behind for your information then, you hear . . ." He slapped his backside viciously but somehow grandly. "And how do I know but what he put a whole bottle of turpentine up my ass to boot. . . . You and old Irene are crazy for details, aren't you. . . . Now does that satisfy you or shall I go up to the turret on the house and shout to the whole countryside showing my bare behind how he did it and on whose graveside it was did, and so forth . . . And how he said, 'How does it feel to have someone give it to you where the fur is short! . . .' "

It was really Sidney who acted like the one who had been raped and torn and whipped with the riding crop and sent home shamed and bare. Even Gareth let up after a while with his sarcasm and biting lip when he saw Sid's gloom and pain.

He sat there again like some old pooped lawyer who is trying to get all the facts and details together before going into the court room, memorizing particulars and exact words and phrases from the "crime."

Then coming out of his reverie, he gave Gareth a searching cool look as he saw again with incredulous wonder that the boy was "better," if by better one meant collected and clear-eyed if irritable, and manly, sharp and nasty, sneering and proud, the way a young man in the country probably ought to be. And maybe like a tiger that first feels the coming of his claws.

Only, Sidney knew in his bones, he was ruined all over again and this time forever. "I mean," Sidney mumbled now to himself, "what can that young fellow think about or hold on to, if through Brian McFee, who was sent by Roy, he was hit by a train, and now he has been dishonored on Brian's grave and sent home like side-bacon on a horse for us to maybe bury or keep hid in the attic. . . . I mean what is to become of him now? . . . What is to become of any of us, if you ask me . . ."

"There is no way, Gareth," Sidney now raised his voice, "no way out, that is, but that I go to him, but killing ain't enough and won't put nothing back together again. I am in fact so riled I can't feel nothing. No," he said, putting his index finger on the veins in his wrist, "nothing, nowhere . . . I feel I have turned to cool air. . . . But wait now" (at a sign of impatience from his friend) "hear me out, I will go there of course . . . Maybe I should walk there naked and just present myself like that . . . But I have to think what I am to say. I can't just walk into the house of a man with so much blood on his hands and say, *'I guess this is your last visit from anybody, Roy, in this world anyhow.'* But what punishment is fit for the likes of him, after all? And how can I do it . . . ? Which is why I got to go over it all carefully like memorizing the lines in a play . . ."

Turning down the counterpane which had slipped over Gareth's mouth, Sidney touched the boy's lips with his and then beseeched:

"Tell me how to punish him, Gareth, and I will . . . I can't think of a way. . . ."

Gareth closed his eyes, then opened them at once.

"Do you hear what I say, Garey?"

"Yeah, of course I hear . . . Shut up while I think, though . . ."

"There ain't nothing bad enough for him I know of . . ."

"Oh yes there is."

"Then why don't you tell me."

"I will whisper it in your ear, Sidney . . . Bend over . . ."

With some trepidation, Sidney put his ear to Gareth's mouth, but sat motionless as he listened to the few words that came out. He went very white.

"You command me to do that, do you?" Sidney said after a silence.

"If you are a man, yes I do . . . If you love me, yes I do . . ."

Sidney stood up.

"All right then if that is your command and your wish, I am your man."

"And don't come back without you do it, hear . . . ? I don't want to see you again if it ain't done . . ."

Raising his arm sleepily, he saluted Gareth. It was not in irony. Then puzzled at such a gesture coming unbidden from himself, he rushed out of the room.

Sidney stood for a long time outside Gareth's room, but he was not thinking about the command so much as he was about the man he was now commissioned to kill. He went downstairs and into the seldom-used parlor and sat in a large heavy chair with gold filigree hanging from it every which way and armrests large enough for a giant.

Roy Sturtevant, he almost pronounced the words aloud, the scissors-grinder, the son of generations of renderers, had sent him his life. Brian McFee, prison, Gareth, his nameless fear, his constant thinking of him, always him, thinking perhaps at the same time of scissors, knives, rendering, the grave, and a kind of glimpse of some sunless world beyond which never ends, but like his thoughts, are constant as immortality.

Gareth's "punishment" at the railroad crossing, unbelievable, even at times ridiculous, lay at the door of the renderer, as was Brian's "murder," but Gareth and Brian and he himself, the "football hero" and "gas-pump attendant" in his foe's savage sarcasm, they were all, he saw now, only envelopes belonging to Roy Sturtevant inside of which was concealed a message only the owner understood.

Yet he felt that Gareth and Brian meant nothing to Roy. One could not even say that Brian McFee had led Sidney astray, or ruined Gareth since from the beginning it was Roy who had power over Sidney from the day he had extended the luxurious handkerchief when in the eighth grade he had lain unconscious and bleeding in the black youth's arms, the handkerchief which had staunched his blood was also itself an envelope which contained the same message: *You will always be mine and your shed blood seals this pact.* The black youth had sensed something of all this too, for looking back at Roy, he had said: *"It would be you who turned up now, wouldn't it. Don't surprise me none at all."*

"So what are you going to do about it?" It was Gareth's lips which pronounced this constantly, hounding him that day and the next, for the invalid himself never said anything again about his "command."

"Plenty, Gareth. In time," Sidney's own eyes and lips would give answer to his loved one's mute and querulous wonder.

"In time! There ain't no time for such a disgrace. He has to die now, and you know it."

So spoke Gareth's silent face in response.

Finally, though, Sidney went into Gareth's room, kissed his hair, and this time spoke aloud: "If it was a stranger, Gareth, he would be dead by now at my hands. But I feel we are dealing with someone outside of human jurisdiction . . ."

Gareth broke away from his lover angrily.

"I am just having the scales fall from my eyes . . . He has been after me all my life as if almost he was me. . . ." At this thought he bent over double for a sudden sharp pain perhaps from his having run up the stairs so desirous to see the person he now loved so vehemently. "So you see, for both our sakes, I can't rush into it like I was dealing with any whichever human being. For no, oh no, he ain't that . . ."

"He's a man like any other. I've seen him cut and bleed right here in my stable."

"I wonder."

"Here he has done this to me in a graveyard, has broke me" (here the thrilling tenor of his voice escaped from the room to go reach beyond the house and the barns and even the little foothills and lose itself in the wind), "and you talk like maybe he was . . . he was . . ."

"Go ahead, Garey, finish your sentence, why don't you?"

Instead Gareth buried his head in his hands and then kept shaking his head imprisoned in his fingers like the pendulum of one of Irene's heirloom clocks.

"You know, Garey, you feel like me he is more than human and can't be dealt with like any other man . . . I know now he holds my life in the hollow of his hand."

"Then let me kill him!" Gareth took down his hands and rose. As he spoke he tore off his dressing gown and stood naked in front of Sidney, who folded him against his chest.

"If you won't, I will . . . I will kill him," the boy extricated himself from the other's embrace.

"We got to plan it, Garey, plan careful . . ."

"And how long is that going to take? Till the snow falls again next October?"

" 'Twill be before snow. You can count on that . . ."

But turning away from Gareth he wandered over to the huge window out of which one saw the mountains still resplendently white. A thrill ran down his spine and legs, a fear that what he really might do if he did not exert all vigilance and caution would be to go to the very sheds where Roy's Grandad had rendered, and call to him, *"I am reporting in on account of I can't run no more. Hear? The tendons in my ankles have give out, the dust won't move under my feet no more, my lungs won't take breath from the air, nor any other organ of my body run right on account of after all—but why tell you?—you have dictated everything and all from the beginning, so here I am to give myself up . . ."*

Even though it was April it kept snowing. The spring flowers were all white with it, the sweet violets and the jack-in-the-pulpits and the maidens tress.

Sidney got out his football shoes and fixed them up a bit for walking. Then he threw them away and took out plain dress shoes that looked incongruous with the kind of rough corduroy pants he wore, but he kept them on. He had some chewing tobacco and he took that along though he didn't much care for it anymore. He had never smoked, like many men who chew don't.

"I don't know what I will say to him," he went on with his soliloquy which now even Gareth's presence did not stop. "That is, what does one say to a man who has been watching you all your life."

He felt, though he could not say it outright, that the word that was falling like drops of gall on his tongue, was *prince*. Not all princes he had read about in old books of legends are beautiful and noble and carry their head high, and his mind went back to his old English teacher who had said once when they were studying words: *"All the word* prince *means is first. And* chief," the teacher had gone on (she had looked suddenly in turn at both Sidney and Roy, and this was to be the only lesson he had ever remembered from school except perhaps another piece of until now meaningless knowledge which came back to him that King Philip of Macedon had agreed that any part of his body might be hewed off of him provided that with what remained he might live in honor), "chief, *young men, is merely from the Latin meaning* head . . ."

"Treat me then like King Philip!" Sidney had said as his leavetaking that day to a thunderstruck Gareth Vaisey.

Sidney had walked first the four miles to Sycamore Lane Cemetery in the same drizzling snow which had afflicted the countryside for weeks, he had broken open the lock of the cemetery gate in his haste, ignoring the shouts of the sexton, a shriveled-up, bent little man, he walked, or rather ran straight to the grave of Brian McFee, uncovering his head, and then stood staring at the same angel Gareth's eyes had been fixed on as he lay writhing in pain under Roy's abuse and mastery over his body on the poorly tended Irish ivy and wild arbutus.

"I will avenge you, too." He kneeled. "Forgive me, Brian, forgive me because I did care for you . . . Brian, if you see me from some big precipice above or in some bottomless hole somewhere, bless me, Brian, and bring me strength . . . Amen."

Now he walked by a detour which took him another four miles out of his way.

The eagles were soaring even on that bleak and sunless day and of course the hawks and the crows and the ravens were making their infernal complaints, all appearing as if they were mad and disgusted with him too, or smelled the stench of death from his having knelt in the graveyard.

"I will eventually if not now have the strength to go through with it." Sidney had looked up now into the vault of the sky which was without warning suddenly cloudless at that moment and the spring snowshower had abated. "I will surrender to what he feels I owe him, but I want my honor. I have to sleep on that before I go. I will keep my honor. Then I may kill him. But first I will say, *"If I have wronged you, renderer"* (this word so long used in the village was in the end now the only word Sidney could know his enemy by), *"wronged you through the years as you are said to claim, then take something from me, but you must likewise pay me back also for what you have done to Brian and Gareth. There must be restitution."*

Then stopping and looking again into the sky which was rapidly clouding over again, great, thick, ice-heavy clouds falling even upon his mouth and wet chin, he directed his words toward where the sun lay buried: "But it was me pulled the trigger that killed Brian." That was the first time he could admit his guilt, his sorrow, his acknowledgment he was the one, erasing his queer words at the trial *I am not sorry.*

He began to cry for the first time for his deed, a dry tearless kind of weeping that pulled at his ribcage as if it would bust his ribs and crush also his spine.

The ravens and crows flew off at the sound.

"Before I get any further into the territory of the . . . the . . . the . . ." Not daring to finish his sentence, he turned back in the general direction of the Vaisey mansion.

He got to the mansion about nightfall. Irene had gone out though all the lights in the house were on as though a Graduation Ball were in progress.

He pitched forward on a dilapidated purple ottoman which stood always in the hallway, and removed his dripping hat. His hair now was almost as long as the scissors-grinder's, but it was not tied behind with a pink cord. He loosened his belt to make breathing easier, though his belt was already several sizes too big for him, as he was getting sparer and sparer and harder and harder of muscle as though when he was asleep unbeknownst even to himself he went out and chopped wood or lifted the colts or steers above his head.

"Did you do it, Sidney?" It was Gareth's voice of course. He was leaning over the banister from the third floor.

"Did you kill him, Sidney? On account of if you ain't going to, I am."

"I'll be right up to tell you," Sidney almost roared back.

Upstairs in their room, Sidney tried to take Gareth in his arms, but the boy he felt he loved the best in the world shook him off impetuously.

"You don't ever touch me again till he's a rotting corpse, do you hear? . . . You're in league with him if you ask me . . . Why did you kill Brian after all? Why did the train hit me? . . . It's all his work, but how do I know maybe yours too . . ."

"Gareth, Christ in heaven, that you could even think such a thing pains me beyond words . . . But to utter it . . ."

"Words! You don't have no words. You're an ignoramus. You never amounted to a shitty tinker's damn and I spite the day I ever set eyes on you. . . . Now, see here," he cried, seizing his lover by the throat, "you either kill that son of a bitch or you never set foot in this house again. Now you get." And in his fury he spat, perhaps involuntarily, in Sid's face.

Sidney raised his hand to wipe away the spit, but then his hand fell without touching his face.

Gareth let out a low little moan.

"Supposin' I do kill him. Where will that get us."

Gareth did not look at him partly because Sid's face was still all swimming from where he had spat upon him.

"I'll tell you why," Gareth began again, "it will break the curse he has put on my house." He was calming down a little as he said this, and in a sudden flurry of motion at which Sidney ducked, thinking he was about to strike him, Gareth wiped the other's face free of his spit with a workingman's handkerchief.

"Never you fear. I'll go see him the first thing in the morning."

"Yeah, you say that with so much enthusiasm. You blighter," he began to raise his voice maniacally again. "I hate you all over again. I regret night and day I was ever close to you. I hated your lovemaking. What are you now? What do you stand for? I don't need you. I ain't even sick anymore if I ever was. Who wouldn't be sick being hit by a train and the lone survivor, and my horses all gone but a few broken-down hacks like you, and you to blame for all of it. You take care of him now, God damn you, or maybe I will take care of you both. . . . How do I know you ain't both in cahoots . . . Tell me, are you in league with him? Why is your face gone so white then?"

"Because as I've told you a thousand times it's him is after me. All my life. I've told you that. It's all I get done thinkin' about: *him*. Look, all right. I'll do it, but when I do it, you watch out too . . ."

Sid was halfway out of the room when the "master" called him back:

"Sit down a minute, why don't you."

"I don't have no more to say, Garey . . . I'm said out. Tomorrow I go . . ."

"I may have been too hard on you, Sid. . . . Better not go then, maybe, better forget him. You're right I guess about if we kill him it will only lead to worse things."

138

This unexpected turnabout after the cruel and devastating speeches his loved one had made to him came too late.

"No, my mind's made up, Gareth. Tomorrow at daybreak I'll go over there and do whatever I feel has to be done at that time."

"Come here," Gareth said. "Come on over here I say and hug me."

"I don't belong to you anymore . . . You killed what I felt for you by talking like you did . . . I can't stand harsh treatment."

"Have you found somebody else better to your taste then?" He spoke without his usual sneering snotty tone. He sounded in fact shaky and a bit hysterical.

"I guess I realize . . . I guess, Gareth, after all . . . Well . . ." Sid flailed his hat around in his hands, and his own saliva fell now copiously from his mouth and on the hand that held his hat. "I guess anybody that has devoted his life to waiting and hounding me, spying and surveying me, spooring and tracking me, maybe he is the one that I should go over to."

"So you are in cahoots."

"Not at all, and never was, and you know it. But how can you hide and sneak and run from one that has nothing else in his life to do but be after you. When all's said and done, I'm all he devotes himself to, don't you see."

"No, I don't."

"Then how can I explain it. I can't even explain it to myself. But think of the cost and the extravagance and the outgo and all. I mean who ever heard of a man that done nothing but think of another man and the other man hardly ever said more than *Good morning* to him."

"That's not quite accurate, for the other man as you call yourself struck the valedictorian in the face on his Graduation

Exercises night. Ain't that more than a *good morning* maybe?"

"You're hard on me today, all right, Gareth, just like you said you were . . ."

"You don't love me anymore, Sid."

Sidney moved his lips, and walked a step nearer to his friend.

"I mean, Sid, you don't love me as much as the renderer loves you."

"I love you though."

"But it ain't enough. Not for me. I want to be loved all-out like he does you."

"Don't say that," Sid cried in true agony, "when you know I'm going to kill him for you . . ."

"Now see here, Sid . . . If you kill him you must kill him for and only for yourself. I don't have no claim on you either so far as killing the son of a bitch is concerned . . ."

"Gareth, do you know somethin'? You're well now. You're a cured boy. You don't need no caretaker or nurse or nothing . . . I bet you could ride a thoroughbred around the race track now."

"What do you mean, I'm cured, you dumb son of a bitch . . . Don't you know I'm crazy and don't you know I'm crazy in love with you . . . ? What's cured about that . . . ?"

Gareth threw himself into Sidney's arms and, rare for him, covered his caretaker with wet passionate kisses.

"Then why do you hurt me and command me? Now I have to go through with killing him and you know it. You won't love me if I don't kill him . . ." He pushed Gareth away, and when the boy tried to take him in his arms again, Sid cried:

"No, keep your distance . . . Don't you spoil my manhood now I've made up my mind to see him and finish it all with him."

140

"He'll kill you, Sidney, don't you see?"

Then with eyes rolling Gareth cried, "He'll *render* you. In the boiling tubs . . ."

"So then he will, and that will be over in a minute."

"Don't you love me no more at all, Sid? . . . You can at least say that."

Gareth stretched out his arms to him like someone on the docks will to a person on a moving ship.

"I'll tell you tomorrow maybe," Sidney answered, and turned his back on him.

The night before the day which brings this story to an end, Roy Sturtevant had been smoking grass steadily all the twenty-four hours before, strong good stuff which made the larynx hoarse and brought sweat out on his palms, and finally made him not see too clearly.

He was sitting in his upholstered best chair with the massive armrests, and then suddenly he couldn't see at all. He waited for a few minutes, and then like an automatic lamp which comes on at dusk, he could see, only he was looking at Brian McFee who stood before him in the Sunday clothes he was buried in. His larynx was so spoiled from weed he could not say anything.

Brian drew near him. He had forgotten how beautiful Brian had been. He had forgotten especially how thick and mahogany his curly hair fell over his smooth white forehead, the furious beet-red of his cheeks and lips, the dimple on his chin. Only his eyes looked different, but perhaps the light and his own condition made them appear only as deep crevices without reflection or movement.

Brian took hold of his right arm and then touched several places on his brow and countenance, and then bowing down he embraced his knees and then his feet.

He did not think he heard Brian speak, but he was sure he gave him a message. The renderer then got back his voice and begged the visitor not to make such conditions, he who had never begged of anybody before .... But as he realized very clearly, he was being commanded by someone who had "gone before" and whose command was law. Roy Sturtevant might command by the laws of this world, but not by the laws of the world to which Brian McFee now belonged.

So he agreed, Roy did. What else was there to do.

"Is there never to be any end of my punishment?" Roy cried out at last after he had gone over the "command" many times with his visitor. "Ain't I ever going to be forgiven either?"

He looked up and there was nobody there.

But there had been somebody, for all over the floor lay dead flowers, geraniums and the leaves of myrtle and pine cones fresh from the grave, and the imprint of brand new shoes.

Roy Sturtevant was in a big tub such as people used to employ for their children especially before indoor plumbing, taking his first bath in about ten years when Sidney De Lakes rapped at the screen door—the storm door was open and the glass broken.

Roy had already emptied the water four times, and was about to get up and empty it again. The water was the color of dark brown river water after a heavy downpour, the kind of water one would expect to find frogs or tadpoles floating around in, but there was, to make up for this lack, pieces of old leaves and other tiny vegetation which had come off from the soles of his feet.

He was so surprised to see this visitor he stood up stark naked in front of him. Then he started to reach for a big white Turkish towel, but his arms were not long enough and Sidney went over and reached it for him.

"So," Roy Sturtevant began, and then he wiped his mouth free from the suds which had gathered over it, "Sidney."

"I promised Gareth," Sidney got out, and almost lunged toward his enemy. "I'm reporting in," he mumbled inaudibly.

They seemed like the first words ever addressed by the football hero to Roy Sturtevant, who went on rubbing himself, going over last his ears till they were beet-red.

"On whose say-so did you say you was here?" Roy inquired. "On account of I ain't required nobody to have you report. I never heard of nobody reporting here and you know it."

"I lied when I said Gareth," Sidney changed his first statement. "I come on my own . . . Still, *their* hands are pushing me too . . . By 'their' I mean not only Gareth and his Dad and brothers but Brian, Brian McFee . . ."

"See here," Roy stumbled out of the tub at the sound of the last name. He shivered badly.

Sidney's eyes widened perceptibly at the appearance of the renderer, all sinews, veins, tendons, the bones themselves almost touchable in places from the regimen he had pursued and which vetoed any hint of fat accumulating on his body.

"I don't believe," the renderer got his voice at last, "in fact I am sure Brian and Gareth would never send somebody else in their place . . . They'd come on their own . . ." He shuddered violently.

"So then I have come to surrender to you."

Roy Sturtevant stood there still naked as he had been born. Then moving like a great cat he hurried over to a stool on which his pants were resting and stepped into them, and threw a T shirt over his chest. His hair he continued to work into the towel.

"You don't deny, do you," Sidney went on somewhat deliriously, his tones very like a baritone solo rather than a speaking voice, "don't and can't deny you have been stalking me all my life. I wonder you was not present when I was born. I feel you have supervised my every breath."

"But why come now?" Roy wondered. "When all's finished and done with. . . . I mean you could have come when you was in the eighth grade and needed me so bad, and I would have helped you night and day with your lessons, your fractions, long division, proportion, and Caesar's *Commentaries* and all the rest you could not ever get straight in your head. . . ." Roy thought a while and then looked down at himself. "My body must have known you was comin' on account of I have bathed like for being laid out in the Greenbrier Funeral Parlor."

"I have been ordered to kill you at least twice, that's for sure." Sidney went on like a windy echo.

Roy grinned on hearing this and began putting salve on his feet.

"You know you deserve death if for only what you done to Gareth." He was trying to feel anger, and then explaining this failure to feel it to his enemy he said, "I have been mad for too long at you to show you now how mad I am . . . Yet I don't feel nothin' when I see you at present. Why is that?"

"Then why don't you go home and think over what it is you plan to do to me if you should report again."

But as the renderer said this, he drew in his breath, preventing himself from screaming only by biting his lips for between himself and the football star he saw Brian McFee dart

144

across his line of vision and then vanish.

"I could never get here again, Roy, for one thing. Once is all I could summon up the strength for." Sidney was speaking unaware of the tumult in the mind of the other man.

"It's that bad, huh?"

Roy put on his socks and heavy high shoes and laced them unsteadily, drowsily.

"How can you be sure as you phrase it, De Lakes, I have been after you all your life? I mean what proof have you?"

"I don't have no proof and don't require or need none. Least ways not for you, who knows it all. I know you have plagued me!"

As Sidney shouted out this last sentence he half-rose, and then slumped down as it was becoming more clear now that he was at last in the presence of his tormentor, that he was actually speaking to the one who had done everything against him, who had in sum dictated his life.

"If you couldn't do simple eighth- and ninth-grade arithmetic and algebra—for I cheated on all the tests for you till you passed—well then how can you prove I have it in for you."

"I already answered that . . . You have haunted me. All my life! You are the one!" It was all he could get out.

Then raising his eyes and his voice he cried out in tones which reached his opponent like flaming steel: " 'Twas you killed Brian McFee!"

Roy Sturtevant laughed, but he laughed too loud and too long for it to be convincing as laughter. Then quieting down he inquired: "If I was to tell you you could be rid of me, would you do it?"

"I have to!" Sidney cried. "I have to be rid of you . . . . Now I see you and how strong you are, I know that . . ."

"Good, good . . . Did it ever occur to you though that I might want to be rid of you also?"

Sidney bent his head down now into his two outstretched palms.

"That never crossed your mind?"

"No."

"Why didn't it?"

"Because it was you who persisted. You know it. I didn't do nothing to egg you on."

"How can you be so sure of that, Sidney?"

"Sidney! He calls me Sidney!" He began to weep deliriously.

"I mean," Roy began volubly, "since you were so dumb all your life in everything, couldn't do simple math or Latin, failed in all you undertook except when you were a football star—you did that good didn't you? Well, how do you know then being such a numbskull though so handsome, that you *didn't* do something to egg me on?"

"I don't follow you."

"Listen then to how you egged me on." He rose and took Sidney's face gently in his hand. "Just by existing you did. Everytime you passed by me you threw off energy enough to make me want you forever. You commanded *me* by just your breathing . . . Like you do now."

"Then how can I stop it?"

"I think there is a way."

"Then tell me how, unless . . ."

"Unless, hell . . . There is this way and this way only."

"I can't kill you even for Gareth . . . I will not kill again! I love him but not that much." He sobbed shamelessly now. "I am not a killer."

"You killed Brian McFee."

"I will not kill you even to be free . . . No."

"Even with a mock-killing?"

Sidney blinked at him through his tears.

"Supposin' you were to nail me naked to the barn door all night, say, and then the next day at sunup you brought Brian McFee to see what you had done, owin' to the fact you claim I killed him through you and so he ought to be present . . ."

"Brian is in his grave, you low son of a bitch."

"But he could be brought out of his grave."

"No!"

Roy had been walking up and down the room as he spoke, and now he approached Sidney De Lakes and took his left hand in his right hand.

"Don't touch me, Sturtevant. Don't, don't . . ."

Roy put his mouth on Sidney's and the latter shivered violently; men have shivered less violently at the moment of death from some pestilential fever.

"Kiss me, Sidney . . . If you want to be free."

"I'm kissin' you," Sidney said between his sobs. His face was wet from tears.

"Let me drink your tears. I ain't never drunk tears."

"Kill me, Roy, why don't you. I don't care. You can kill me, then render me, nobody will know."

"I don't want to kill you. Never wanted to." He went on kissing Sid's face assiduously all over, his kisses drying it of his tears.

He took out Sidney's penis and bent Sidney's own face over his penis, and said, "Cry on your own cock, Sidney. Go on, cry on it. Refresh your cock."

"Kill me or let me go," he blubbered, his face held against his own sex.

Pulling up his head with his hands so that Sidney faced him again, Roy said: "If you go home without doin' what I say you won't never be free of me ever . . ."

"I can't dig up the man I shot, for God's sake . . . Have some pity or decency."

Sidney rose and then threw himself down on the floor, face forward.

Roy bent down over his prostrate visitor, brought his face upwards, then took Sidney's penis into his own mouth, holding it briefly.

"No, no," Sidney cried. "I can't bear it, I can't, I can't."

"Will you do what I say then?" he fulminated.

"I will try . . . But for God's sake don't make love to me . . . Kill me first . . ."

"Tryin' ain't good enough."

He began sucking him again.

"Yes, I'll do it . . . I'll do it, Roy . . ."

"But if you don't do it right, Sidney," Roy said, getting up, "I will do something so bad to you you will remember it for a billion years in hell."

Sidney nodded.

"I say, will you do it now if I let go of you," for he still held on to his penis with his hand.

"I'll do it."

He pushed Sid's penis back into his trousers, and buttoned him up.

"I'll need some shovels and a pickaxe and stuff," Sidney spoke.

He began to sob more violently and then he screamed once or twice in such a hideous way even Roy looked aghast. Quieting down then a little, he asked, "Must I do it, Roy?"

He kept asking this over and again.

"Yes, Sidney, if you would be free . . ."

"All right, now listen to me," Roy began, for he knew what he was about to say, what he had indeed been commanded now to say were words that would not be believed, would not indeed be thought of as having been correctly heard.

"After you gather up the picks and shovels and other tools, just before you go off to the cemetery, I want you to nail me to the barn door. Do you hear?"

Sidney waited. He nodded slowly. Then he went over to the screen door, opened it quickly, and vomited out onto the geraniums and petunias and morning glories all growing wild in disarray. He wiped his mouth on the back of his hand and came back on in.

Roy was busy with collecting the nails out of a box, and had brought out two hammers, a large heavy one, and another of lesser weight but hefty utility.

He took off all his clothes, and then picked up a revolver which had been resting, unseen by Sidney, on a small commode.

He pointed the gun at Sid and they walked over to the great barn, newly painted and shining bright, and Roy pulled open the largest of the barn doors.

"This is the door you are to nail me to, do you see?"

Sidney nodded. Roy did not know whether to be relieved or angered by such calm compliance.

But then after this wooden docility, Sidney kneeled down in front of the renderer, saying, "Release me, or kill me. I can't, I can't go through with it."

"The only way you can release yourself is to nail me fast to the barn door. Now I will give you some dope to drink if you want it, but I got to be nailed there, and you got to bring Brian to see me in the morning. Otherwise, you won't never be free of me. . . . Is that clear now?"

"I don't know, I don't know," Sidney kept muttering.

"Well, stand up, then, for if you don't do it I am going to shoot you. Understand?

"All right. Now I want you to bathe my right wrist and arm and my right foot and thigh with this alcohol I brought along." Roy took out the stopper from a large bottle, and Sidney listlessly rubbed these portions of his body with the solution.

Then Roy pointed to the nails lying all ready in a row on some white cloth beside the two hammers.

"Now you nail me to the door just like you was as smart as the next fellow, get it? You owe it to both of us, Sidney. Nail the son of the renderer to the barn door. You know you want to. A slap was not enough that night of the Graduation Exercises."

Suddenly a great cry came out of Sidney's chest which made even the scissors-grinder wince a bit. Sid had the nails in the palm of his left hand, and then after a long wait of pure silence he raised the heavier of the two hammers.

The first nail went through Roy's wrist with more ease than he had thought possible.

The renderer went pale, especially in the mouth, but no sound escaped from him. The blood perhaps spoke for him as it jetted about everywhere staining Sidney's shirt and hands, spurting even on his hair.

Then driven by some force unknown to him, Sidney had soon nailed his arm, the foot and ankle with several heavy nails to the barn door. In his haste to hammer he stumbled over a small box which spilled out more nails.

Sidney then drew back from his handiwork. Roy appeared to have passed out, but then all at once he opened his eyes again. He was badly stained with blood which kept on running, trickling, even gurgling.

"Then in the morning," Roy began to speak, but stopped. "In the morning you bring Brian, don't forget," he got out somehow.

"I think your arm needs a couple more nails," Sidney spoke, his mouth open and working furiously.

Sidney pounded the extra nails in with vehement concentration.

He waited as if marveling at the many little streams of blood coming out of the body of Roy Sturtevant, like many little brooks and creeks swollen by sudden cloudburst.

"Then I will be back in the A.M. with Brian McFee," Sidney announced with his mouth almost directly over the closed eyes of the man nailed to the barn door. "At the first flush of day I will bring him to you."

Sidney De Lakes had been a high-diver in high school among his other athletic accomplishments, and his coach had wanted him to try for a scholarship to a large school later on, and become one day, who knows? an Olympic star.

Even though he dived with the beauty and precision already of a laureate athlete he hated diving and hated water.

Now as he drove off in Roy Sturtevant's truck with the pickaxe and other tools for digging, headed for the cemetery, he felt again as he had when he had dived into the pool to the plaudits and huzzahs of his coach. Actually when he had seen the admiration and even love on the face of the young man who had taught him to dive and swim so superbly he felt there was no need to go on and work harder to be an Olympic victor. His coach's admiration and closeness completely satisfied his ambition.

Now again as he faced the imposed task of digging up Brian McFee he felt a new and infallible coach was commanding him to dive into some bottomless abyss, and he feared it much more than death itself as he feared more than death putting the first nail in the flesh of his enemy the renderer's son, but then, having put in the first nail he had wanted to put in more, he had wanted as a matter of fact to cover entirely the scissors-grinder's body with nails so numerous that he would look like he was clothed in an iron suit composed of shiny little silver heads.

But he had discovered something else, as when from perilous heights of diving he had discovered he loved not the sport but the coach, now he saw not in a blinding flash but in a calm recognition that as he had watched the contempt of the renderer for the pain and mutilation he was inflicting on him, he loved Roy Sturtevant in the same way he loved his coach, who had also commanded him to accomplish the impossible.

In almost the blinking of an eye then Roy Sturtevant had become his coach. There was no scissors-grinder or renderer anymore, with blackened fingers and dirty ears, there was merely the young man bleeding and nailed to an old Pennsylvania-style barn who was waiting for his pupil's return with Brian McFee whom they had both loved equally.

So the wheel had come full circle, his past was blotted out along with most of his memory, all that remained to him therefore was this new coach bleeding and heroic against the barn door. So, he would show him Brian McFee, he would take the nails out, and then hold him in his arms for he would be his, they would both be one another's forever. Roy would guide and keep him, he would not let him go wrong again, they would not part from one another ever after having only at last been united pursuant to so many devious detours and windings, as souls long separated from each other by the world's vicissitudes are said to enter paradise linked arm in arm.

It was about an hour and a half till daybreak when Sidney went upstairs to Gareth's room. Gareth was sitting up, which gave Sid a shock for he resembled so very much Brian McFee who was also sitting up by the driver's seat down below waiting for Sidney to drive him back to Roy and the un-nailing.

"Did you kill him? You've been gone long enough to kill a army."

Sidney kept staring at him, marveling at the resemblance, and feeling dizzy by reason of the teeter-totter effect of his running now to Roy, then back to Gareth, and then all over again from one to the other.

"It's all settled," Sidney spoke in the dreamy manner which had become habitual with him of late. He slumped down into the armchair and his hat fell off at his feet.

"What's the meaning of all that earth on your shoes and pants?" Gareth wondered.

Then after studying his lover: "Did you kill and bury him already?"

Sidney's lips began to form the word *Yes,* but then coming up with a start he answered, "Roy ain't dead yet, no."

Then panicking at Sidney's peculiar behavior and his flushed cheeks, Gareth cried: "Where did you leave him then?"

"He's nailed to the barn door."

Gareth let out a sound like a balloon being burst, then jibed: "You're stoned, ain't you, you dumb shitass. . . . You didn't do nothing to him I bet."

"Oh, no? . . . Well, Brian's down there in the truck, for your information. We're going back, him and me, to Roy's place at daybreak and then I'm goin' to take the nails out."

Gareth shook his head, a volley of oaths and curses came out but not so much aimed at Sidney as perhaps at the powers which had bestowed on him life and breath.

"I promised him," Sidney was going on, "I would bring Brian back so he could see him nailed to the barn."

Gareth got out of bed and came over and looked at Sidney close all over. Then stooping down Gareth picked Sidney's hat up and put it on his head, and as he put the hat heavily over his head, his long hair began to fall down but did not fall as long or as far as usual because it was secured this time by a familiar pink cord in the back.

"I'll see about this," Gareth admonished him, "and I will be going along to find out if you are totally in-sane or whether . . ."

He pulled on his pants and ran noiselessly down the long staircase. He opened the screen door, then the storm door, and went out to where the truck was parked. He was gone a long time, in fact Sidney meantime had fallen asleep and had begun to snore.

When Gareth came back into the room he walked like some crippled old man of ninety. He could barely help himself into bed and put his upper body under the counterpane. He made queer little sounds almost like that of a quail when he senses the shadow of a hawk over it. Then he began to cry.

Sidney woke up. "Did you take a peek?" he wanted to know.

154

Gareth cried on.

"Why don't you shut up," Sidney said indifferently. "You might wake up everybody."

"He don't look . . . rotten," Gareth got out now, the horror of what he had seen not yet having completely reached him. "He looks . . . fresh . . ."

"I think," Sidney began swallowing convulsively, and then he took off his hat and looked inside the crown, "I reckon . . . the coach . . . must have embalmed him lavishly on the sly."

"He looks alive!" Gareth moaned.

"I think you're right."

"But who is the coach, Sid?" Gareth mumbled, rising up in the bed and loosening the covers.

"Why, *him* of course."

Gareth Vaisey did not ask more, he was weeping silently now but spasmodically.

"I shouldn't have told you to," Gareth kept repeating. "It was my fault . . ."

"No, Garey, no." Sidney went over to the bed and sat down on it, but the younger man drew violently away from him.

"Kiss me, Garey, please kiss me."

"No, no . . . I think I will kill myself now."

"Kiss me, please." He took hold of Gareth and kissed him wetly, bringing the boy afterwards against his breast.

"I got to be there at the first flush of day, Gareth. I promised him, you know."

"Will Roy be dead too when you get there?"

"I don't think he will ever die, if you ask me."

"What did you say you did to him?" Gareth was wiping his eyes with the freshly laundered pillowcase.

"Roy said I had to do it, that's why I called him the coach who always made me do (remember?) things I couldn't do, like climb without ever having practiced that big rope that led up to the gym ceiling, go through all those spine-twisting tricks on the horse, run round the stadium till I puked for an hour from my lungs being turned inside out, so when this new coach says, *'You have to nail me to the barn door if we are ever either of us to have any peace or rest or go on our separate ways, for this has been going on for nearly ten years, long enough for a man to marry and be raising his own kids,'* I said, *'I can't do it. I mean my fingers won't obey me even if my brain said* Do it,' and the New Coach said, *'Well, I'm in your brain then and your fingers and your heart and your kidneys and bladder and all your organs put together, see? and I do say,* Nail me to the door, *and save the both of us . . . But fetch Brian with you . . . ,'* 'Brian is dead, you motherfucker!' 'All right, fetch him just the same!' he answers. *'Don't you believe in death?'* I yelled at him. *'No,'* he answers, *'and I don't believe in time neither . . .'* "

"So I will go back with you then to Sturtevant's place," Gareth said very quietly, more like he used to speak when he had been very sick and was so dependent on Sidney.

"Don't see any reason why you can't. . . . After all I just have to do them two things, show him Brian, if he's still alive, and remove the fucking nails."

"That shouldn't take too long, should it, Sid?"

"No, I expect not," he answered. Then he kissed Gareth on the forehead, touched his lips to his cheek, and after a wait put his mouth on Gareth's mouth like he was tasting a plate of fresh-picked cherries. Then catching sight of the first few streaks of the dawn, Sidney jumped up and ran down the stairs three at a time.

"Wait for me, wait up, Sidney. You promised!"

Gareth climbed on the side of the car which was already in motion and the rifle he was all of a sudden carrying with him went off twice. Sidney stopped the truck.

"Get in, I had most forgot about you when I seen the sun coming up. . . . Get in the back on the floor on account of Brian should ride right beside me, don't you think . . ."

Gareth jumped in the back of the truck holding his rifle.

"He don't smell like he's dead, and he looks just about the same as when we knew him . . . Only he smells of something sure enough . . ."

"I can tell you," Sidney said, "I don't know if I am dreamin' or dead myself or what . . . I seem to be drivin' this truck, that's about all I know for sure. If he ain't there nailed to the door I will know I have dreamed it all and am back in jail probably. I won't care by then. In fact jail will be a good rest after what I been through. Old Vance should have let me rot in jail, always told him that anyhow. I sort of belong in jail. . . . But when he begun to talk to me, Roy, you know, and persuaded me to nail him to the barn door, I sort of thought, 'Well, if I can't be in jail maybe the next best thing would be to give myself up, and to live locked up with the scissors-grinder and be done pretending I ever was out free . . .'"

"See here now, Sid," Gareth began and just as he spoke he caught a whiff of the dead boy in the front seat that made him stop and then choke.

"Go on, have your say, Gareth."

Choking and gagging into his pocket handkerchief now, the Vaisey boy struggled to get the words out. At last he shouted: "You wouldn't leave me for the renderer would you? Was that what you were sayin' back in the house?"

"Well, what if he commands me again. I ain't never been

commanded so firm before, Garey, like he done for instance when he said I should nail him. Do you think I would nail anybody like that on my own? What do you think I am anyhow, huh? No way. I wouldn't do that ever on account of I don't see how I did it even now. If I did it. If he's there, that is, when we go back and we ain't both locked up in some lunatic asylum dreaming this whole thing."

"You was stoned, that's all."

"Not really. No, sir, I was not."

"You're always stoned anyhow, and you know it . . . So you nailed him stoned . . . But I know something, and if what I know proves accurate, you watch out, De Lakes, God damn you watch out."

"Meaning what?"

"Just this. If I see you have gone over to this renderer son of a bitch, you better take cover, do you hear?"

"You got to explain yourself better than that if you want me to understand you."

"You just missed the detour to Roy's, you dumb crud. Now turn back and head south . . ."

Sidney began to swear now and to sound a little more like himself, and wheeled about and then turned down a little dirt side road, but then presently he got stuck in what was left of a big snow pile, and had some trouble getting unstuck before proceeding on the new road. When he got to a clear part of pavement again he put on the gas and went most ninety miles an hour.

"Did you hear what I was telling you, driver, before you fucked up our itinerary."

"Hear that spoiled snot complain, would you! Look. See here . . . When you have been through what I have, what no man who ever drew breath has done been through before, why do you want to eat my ass out about missing a little road sign, huh? I ask you, Garey . . . You lay off me . . ."

"Listen to me good, Sid, you cheap fucker, now you listen good and proper." He put the muzzle of the gun between Sid's shoulder blades.

"Now you stop that chicken shit, Garey. God damn you."

"Are you listening to me, or will I have to take care of you?"

"How can I help not listening . . . Even Brian McFee here is listening, the loud mouth you are."

"All right then . . . I say if you go over to the renderer I am going to blow your brains out."

Sidney slowed the truck down. Then he came to a full stop.

"Get out, Garey, get your rosy ass up and out."

"I'm in earnest, Sid. If you go over to the renderer I will kill the both of you, mark my words. . . ."

"What's that supposed to mean?"

"I have the feeling you love him. Do you?"

"I think something has happened to me, Garey." Sidney's voice shook now. He sounded like he was praying to an indifferent idol. "Sure enough. I ain't never been commanded so before. I told you that back at the house. You just wait and see how I bet he commands me again. I bet he can command me still nailed to that door."

"You fucked-up hunk."

"I can't help what's happening, Garey. Did I ever seek him out? You tell me."

"Ho, all you ever talked about, thought about, or dreamed about all your life is this renderer guy, if you ask me. You coy little motherfucker. I know what you do to us all. You're a coy faggot, that's all you are, and that's why they throwed you to the cement and fucked you in jail 'cause you act the part of a little coy faggot no matter how tough and all-American you look. You ain't fooled me from the first, but I can tell you one thing—if you go over to the renderer, it's your life, De Lakes . . . I aim to kill both of you if I see any shit treachery, is that clear?"

Sidney started the motor. He was even whiter than he had been back at the house, and his hands were shaking.

"Take that rifle from between my shoulders, you dizzy cocksucker. On account of I can't drive with no gun pointed at my lungs."

Gareth pulled the gun away.

"Brian McFee is beginning to stink like a bona fide real dead man, if you ask me," the Vaisey boy said after a long silence in which Sidney drove his car at full speed, with screeching of brakes and punishing of tires and sudden break-neck turns as in a last-lap car race.

"Oh, it's only cause the air is getting warm, Garey. . . . I don't dare look at him again. I looked at him once, and I tell you something . . . I kissed him." He slowed down when he said this because his hands were shaking again.

"Yeah, you had him fooled too," Gareth scolded. "He thought you loved him, poor baby . . . And all the time your heart belonged to this scissors-grinder which to hear you talk was your worst enemy. . . . Well, we are going to see in a few minutes who is in charge here . . . Or the blood will flow like spring freshets, you can count on that. You cheap four-flusher, you God damn low-down flirt, you . . . I ought to choke you to death right over the steering-wheel. Supposed to tend and care for me, was you? Made love to me and told me I was your only one, and all the time since the eighth grade you have been slave to this unwashed turd goes by the name of the renderer."

"He don't render and never did, and it was you explained it to me first. And he explained it all over to me again. It was his old Grandpa that done it. He ain't never been in the rendering business and you know it."

"But it was 'cause he had the stain on him of bein' a renderer that you never spoke to him all through school, that you held yourself aloof from him which was what drove him crazy in the first place when all the time he loved you from the time he was thirteen years old. Your coyness drove him crazy and you are the cause of it all. . . . Your nailin' him to the door was the kindest thing you ever done for him. Don't tell me you ain't coy, you slick prick-teasin' stuck-up smartass, you have been teasin' everybody ever set eyes on you from the time you was birthed, you cheap showcase fucking football model, you. You drove all them convicts crazy too in jail I can believe that. I should shoot you here and now and the world would thank me for it, every prison in the U.S.A. would send me a telegram of thanks and appreciation that the coy little flirt of a football hero is plugged and out of service in his coffin . . ."

"You sure are cured, Gareth. You are *well*! You don't need nobody to take care of you or change your diapers anymore. And you know what? I will give you tit for tat, you mutherfucking snot, you was never sick at all. I seen through you. It was just an excuse to get my loving and be safe so you could go on using your Ma as a meal ticket and have my good love in the bargain. . . . I ain't fooled by what Doc calls your psychosomatic malady, hell, no.

You are a cheap playactor, and there ain't an honest hair in your pretty little head . . ."

Gareth put the gun back between his shoulders, but then he removed it almost instantly.

"Never fear, Sid, I am not going to kill you in the car. I want to see how your lover will greet you as you approach him nailed to the barn door. That is, if the nails ain't drunk all his blood and have fallen out . . ."

"I put more nails in him than he asked for, that's for sure . . . He seen that I was carried away. . . . But you know something? He wasn't scared. No, had I started to nail his mouth shut to his brain he wouldn't have said a word in way of protest."

"That's because you've been torturing him all your life. As the hero of the football team, the diver and swimmer, the pure American stock back to the Revolution or before, looking down on the renderer's son like he was some nigger or drunk Indian not good enough to spit on your shoes to shine them. . . . Well the renderer is a thousand times better 'n you and that snot Vance ever was . . . And he had the soul to suffer all these years just like what you have put me through with your no-account loving. You don't know how to love. And you will die, you cruddy bugger, you will die by my gun when I am good and ready."

"Hear him!" Sidney answered.

But there was something to the way he pronounced these two words that indicated he felt satisfaction somehow in what was now happening. At least everything, his entire life, that is, was approaching a showdown, and he felt more exhilarated than had he smoked the best hash or grass. He was at some summit of his own self, and he was, if not happy, at last himself, and then he was also going to take down the man who when all was said and done had loved him the best and who he now believed after all he was in love with. At least he was his "coach," and he had loved perhaps only his coach who had made him a star. He was sure every so often that the renderer was now able to confer the same glory on him, and bind his brows as a victor over some unknown and unheralded ordeal. See how already he had done a great thing by nailing him to the door when no other human command could have forced him so to act.

"We're getting close now to where he lives or at least used to live, so I am putting this gun down—hear?—but it is cocked and ready to blow your brains out if you don't obey me as good or better than you obeyed your lover the scissorsgrinder. . . . So now pull yourself together for the sequel, Sidney De Lakes."

He had hardly said all this before they turned off the road marked Warrior Creek and drove up to the Sturtevant place with its three barns, four farm houses, and the ruins of the old rendering sheds.

"Did you ever see such a sight now! By God, he was telling me the truth for once in his life!"

Gareth said this, for he had been the first to jump out of the truck and run right up to the barn door, and there he was, nailed stark naked just as Sidney had told him he would be.

"Are you dead, Roy? Because you sure look it." (Sidney closed his eyes as he heard this part of Gareth's ranting, and made no sign he was about to come out of the truck.)

"Because," Gareth's voice still reached him, "if you *are* still alive I may aim to shoot you myself and put you out of your misery."

He rubbed his hand over the renderer's chest, and when it

came away smeared with red he wiped his hand lazily on his trousers.

"You let go of my prisoner!" Sidney suddenly shouted, leaning out of the truck window. "I am fulfilling my part of this bargain, and you keep out of it. You hear me? You dry up. I'm sick of you putting the screw on me."

"Would you look at them nails, the size of them, the way they have been pounded in!" Gareth's voice rose over the gray-white landscape, echoing and re-echoing from the empty barns and sheds and unused houses. "Why you are a God damned fiend, Sidney De Lakes." Here Gareth turned, still holding his rifle, which having been pointed at Roy Sturtevant was now aimed in the general direction of the truck.

"Put that damned gun down, you hear, and get over here and help me with Brian, will you?"

For some reason Gareth obeyed Sidney. He put the rifle down by a little fence with cottoneaster vine growing all over it, and sauntered up to the truck.

Sidney, his face flushed, his mouth open, was lifting the dead Brian out of the truck.

"He's heavy as lead for some reason or else I have lost all my strength from hearin' you ravin' and rantin' . . . ."

Gareth made a show of holding his nose.

"You help me with him, curse you, Garey . . . Why don't you behave!"

Gareth took hold of the dead boy and helped Sidney carry him directly in front of where the renderer stood against the barn door. They propped Brian up with a few good-sized boulders that were lying around.

All at once Sidney turned away, doubled up, and began to cry as if somebody had shot him in the belly.

"I ain't dead, Sidney."

(Sidney and Gareth were not certain who said these words and they gazed at one another for what seemed like an eternity, and later on in the hospital jail Gareth Vaisey admitted that he had thought Brian McFee had spoken them, and Gareth had thrown himself as a result on the ground and flailed about like someone having a fit.)

"Was that you who spoke, Roy?" Sidney said cautiously and began walking in the direction of the barn door.

"Who else?" Roy answered back, and opened his eyes.

His eyes were like two stones floating in blood, beautiful and eloquent too. He closed then as soon as he saw Sidney.

Sidney began speaking very close to the renderer: "I done like you told me to, Roy, but it should never have been done if you ask me . . . I hope you are going to be all right, though." He touched his chest with his forefinger and then drew it away streaming with blood.

"Where is Brian?" Roy inquired, his eyes still shut.

"Right in front of you, Roy. Cain't you see him?"

Roy opened his eyes and gradually focused them on Brian. They had placed the dead boy on a mound of earth that might have been—who knows?—once an ant hill.

"How did you get him to sit up like that?" Roy wondered.

"I guess I had to break his back maybe, to tell the truth."

"That's Brian all right," Roy agreed. "I have to hand it to you, De Lakes."

Sidney had closed his own eyes now, and he kept passing his hand forward and backwards over his face.

"I want to take you down from the door now, Roy, and put you to bed. Then I will call the doctor . . . Whatever you command though," he added quickly at a look fearful to behold which came from the renderer.

165

"You have changed, Sidney De Lakes."

"How have I?"

"You are different. Different all around."

Sidney looked back where Gareth lay on the grass very quiet and still.

"I think Gareth had some kind of a fit," Sidney opined.

Sidney began walking in little circles around the hammer with which he had pounded Roy into place. He circled about the hammer as if it was a dangerous animal which might attack him. Then very deliberately he bent over it, and picked it up gingerly. His jaw closed tight.

Then very quickly, almost as though he had leaped upon Roy, he wielded the hammer over the renderer and swiftly pulled out one of the nails. There was a scream of pure agony, then Roy fainted, his head falling to his chest which still swam with little circles of blood.

When Sidney pulled out the next nail the pain must have been so pronounced he came to. Then Roy waited with his eyes open resting on Sidney, and Sidney waited also.

Sidney's face drew closer and closer to that of the renderer. His lips then brushed against the nailed man's beard.

"What was the meaning of that, Sidney?" Roy questioned him.

"Does it have to have a meanin'?" Sidney answered huskily. He touched his face against that of the sufferer and held it there as light as a feather.

"Pull out the rest of the nails."

"Can you take it?" Sidney wondered, his words propelled against the cheek of Sturtevant.

"Well, let me see," Roy said. He began to hemorrhage from his mouth, and Sidney wiped away the blood with his hand.

166

They both waited a lengthy time. Then Roy began again, "Go in the house and in the big kitchen cupboard in the second drawer from the top you will find some medicine with a pink label on it. It's marked *Emergency only, dangerous.*"

"But it ain't poison is it, Roy?" Sidney was touching Roy's damp hair which now covered almost entirely one eye. His hair too was wet with blood.

"What do you care what it is? . . . No, it ain't poison, but even if it was I have already drunk all the poison even old Doc Ulric could prescribe for me . . . So go and get it, or pull out the rest of the nails without you get it. Suit yourself."

Sidney acted as if he could not pull his face away from Roy's, like an insect which has fallen on some intoxicating slippery surface.

Suddenly their lips met, and remained pressed together.

Then they kissed several times. The renderer let out a groan, and pulled away. His head fell down again.

Sidney ran in the back door and rummaged through the commode. He could not lay his hands on any such bottle for many minutes. Then clear behind some heavy lace napkins yellowed with age, it was visible. He looked at it gloomily, took off the stopper and smelled it. He drew away from the odor, gagging. He picked up a glass from the kitchen sink and was about to take it along, then decided the wounded man could drink better from the bottle itself, and put the glass down.

Roy was unconscious, and his entire body swam with gore. Sidney studied him and watched his breathing, took his pulse, and finally opened his left eye and looked at the pupil.

He drank a swallow from the bottle first, and choked on it, but kept it down. Then he managed to waken Roy and had him drink several swallows, but he vomited out the first two. Then he made a renewed effort and this time drank thirstily, and kept the liquid down.

Sidney's eyes moved down to where Roy's cock hung in almost purple folds of flesh, bleeding also as if he had put nails in it, and his testicles which appeared to be naturally large had begun to shrivel up in consonance with the damage and pain done to his arms and legs.

"I'm goin' to pull out the remainin' ones, Roy . . . You hear me, buddy . . . The last ones now, Roy, so bear up . . . Roy?"

Fearful barely human screams then rose from the barn door. The finches and song sparrows made a great fuss from the nearby pear trees and rose in little flocks into the air and winged their way out into the forest toward the west, and the horses whinnied in the nearby second barn and kicked at the siding.

Freed from the last of the nails, Roy fell into Sidney's arms like a young tree will topple directly on you if you have not taken the proper precaution in your having felled it.

The impact from Roy's falling body caused them both to stumble and slip to the earth where they lay facing Brian McFee, whose eyes were open, though they were more or less holes now, and the morning sun had begun deepening the look of rot on his face. Still he looked beautiful and young and, thought Sidney, very much like somebody in the colored plates of the family Bible, maybe Jonathan or Absalom.

Roy coughed up blood from his mouth all over Sidney's hands and arms, but Sid barely noticed it in his rapt study of Brian.

Then rising, Sidney lifted Roy into his arms and carried him carefully to the kitchen entrance, but there, slipping, he fell down with him in his arms, and they lay there together on the thick woolen rug pressed against one another so close that they appeared to be one man with the same common injuries.

Sidney managed to get up again, and carried Roy all the way upstairs, though this staircase if anything was longer and broader than that of Irene Vaisey's. Upstairs he hesitated as to which room he should choose. He selected the king-sized one, though actually Roy slept in the small room at the end of the hall.

He laid the scissors-grinder down on the bed. A toilet and bathroom adjoined the room, where he found a number of clean wash rags and towels. He waited a long time for the water to get warm, looking within the room anxiously as he waited. He picked up two bars of homemade soap, then selected a little wash basin and brought all this into the bedroom.

Sidney bathed the sick man with all the care and finesse which he had acquired from his months of having cared for Gareth. But Roy did not open his eyes during these ministrations.

"I guess that stuff you had in the bottle was the granddaddy of all pain-killers, Roy, for I feel like I'm in a sky of clouds though I didn't begin to drink as much as you."

Sidney waited a while studying the sleeper.

"Can you hear me, Roy?"

He took his pulse again, and then allowed his hand to rest in his.

"Sure I can hear you," Roy replied, but his voice sounded like it was coming from downstairs. "I know all you did and are doing . . . I know it all . . ."

"That's good."

"You think so?" Roy opened his eyes and stared at De Lakes.

"Why did you make me do it, Roy?" he wondered, pressing his hand in an ironlike grip.

"Why did you make me do it?" came the languid weary response.

"You're sassing me, Roy . . . Well, go ahead if it suits you. Sass away if it makes you feel better. I deserve sassin'. I deserve, oh, I don't know what. I am so mixed up, Roy, I don't know who I am . . ."

"Did you ever?"

"Did I ever what? My mind is sort of wandering . . . Know who I am? . . . Oh I don't know . . ."

Sidney made dolorous whinnying sounds like those which had come from the horses awhile back when they had heard their owner scream.

"Everything comes to you in the end," Roy began speaking now while putting his hands through Sidney's hair, gently pulling the strands of thick yellow hair, then rearranging it gently this way, that way, then stroking his head. "By and by it all comes down on a fellow."

"Why did you want Brian to see you nailed?" Sidney mumbled, almost too low for the scissors-grinder to catch.

Without warning, turning away violently, Roy vomited up some more blood.

Sidney patiently, sleepily cleaned the places over which he had hemorrhaged and went then into the bathroom and emptied the basin and brought back fresh water.

Sidney got very calm then. He was looking at Roy's breast steadily. It was the pectorals, he decided, of an Olympic runner. One could see not only all the muscles easily defined as in a school anatomy text, but he felt he could perceive also the veins and arteries and even the marrow of his bones. He leant over and kissed Roy again and again.

The wounded man opened his eyes and looked down at Sidney.

"It's too late, Sidney," he said, scrutinizing the man embracing him.

"No it ain't, Roy . . . You'll get better. See now if I ain't right. You'll mend. Let me call the doctor."

"No," Roy spoke with indifferent emphasis. "I don't want no doctor in my house. I'm a doctor. I know more about the human body than Doc Ulric or a whole college of doctors could learn in another thousand years of study."

"You should have nailed me to the door, Roy," Sidney whispered.

"No, no, that wouldn't have worked. It had to be this way."

"Do you want me to take it in my mouth to show you," Sidney said, for his hand had been slowly moving down toward Roy's sex and now he held it fast.

"No."

"I want to."

"Oh well . . . But just for a few moments. I lost me too much blood to do anything like that."

Sidney put his mouth over the renderer's sex and kept it covered, sucking and kissing and licking obediently, until Roy pulled away from him.

"Not now, not now!"

"That was strong medicine you had in that bottle in the commode, Roy," Sidney spoke after a while. He was resting his head on the renderer's bosom.

"I sure feel it, Sidney, and that is a fact."

"Do you want more?"

"By and by, yes." The renderer's hand plunged then into

Sidney's curls. The football star shivered and shook, and the renderer twirled the curls into fine little threads like gold yarn.

"You'll pull through and be as good as new," Sidney said.

The hot fluid that suddenly fell on his face as he spoke he mistook for a second for more hemorrhaging, but instead he saw it was tears falling on him. They were hotter than blood.

"Put me in those pajamas I never wore and that are in the top drawer of the bureau."

"You have everything you want in the drawers of commodes and bureaus, don't you," Sid said.

It took quite a while to get Roy into his nightclothes, and both the pajama shirt and the trousers were soon stained from all the bleeding which had started up again once he had been moved.

"What time o' day is it getting to be?" Roy said after a long time had passed.

"I'll have to get up and go downstairs to see, Roy. I ain't sure."

"Oh, don't bother. I can see it's afternoon by the way the light falls."

They heard the police sirens in the distance.

Sidney remembered how not too long ago, as a matter of fact, once in prison he had gone into the shower room and had unexpectedly run into a man in there alone, a man he had never liked before and who, to put it bluntly, always smelled like a dog after it has been bathed. But in the dim light of evening, this same man looked like a prince (he had actually murdered five people), his eyes flashing baleful messages of beauty and desire, his body like a bronze statue that breathed and moved almost imperceptibly in its grace. Sidney had gone unasked and taken the man in his arms. They had fallen to the floor and had one another all that night. He had lied to Vance, you see, that "terrible things" had been done to him in prison, or rather he had failed to say that he himself had initiated the "terrible things."

Remembering prison then, he felt he was transported back there, and that the man he had loved so devotedly that evening was again by his side. There was no renderer, or son of a renderer, no scissors-grinder or cistern cleaner or tree surgeon or any of the other vocations attached to his enemy's name, and there never had been any Sidney De Lakes, a football star and gasoline station attendant, for he felt he was back thousands of years ago with this "eternal" lover or husband or sweetheart, whatever name, on whom he now poured out all his love.

Roy Sturtevant was returned thus from time to time from the dark valley into which he had sunk, by these improbable, lavish, even cruel caresses coming from the man who lay beside him.

Roy kept saying from time to time: "You're Sidney, ain't you?"

"Whoever I am, I am yours. I am all yours."

"Then why, if you are him," Roy would repeat after him as if they had both learned these lines, did not understand them, but had to keep repeating them, perhaps for a tape recording in some unknown prison, "why, why did it take you so long then?"

"I don't follow you, Roy . . . What is it you mean?"

"I said, what took you so long . . . ? All the time you have waited to tell me it wasn't hate you had for me after all."

"All I know is I have you now, Roy. You're mine. That's all I know."

"But you're stoned, so maybe it ain't real after all, or won't

173

be tomorrow." He drew back the upper lids of Sidney's eyes as he said this, and looked into them. Then taking his head in his hands he kissed Sidney on the mouth solemnly.

"It's real now, Roy, real also in an hour or so, and 'twill be real tomorrow to boot. Hear?"

"I don't have no tomorrow," the scissors-grinder said. "I'm finished."

The hinges of the door creaked, the door opened, and there stood Gareth with his rifle.

"The state troopers are on the way," he spoke thickly, sullenly. "It's on the radio downstairs . . . They discovered the robbed grave . . ."

Gareth had spoken possibly before he had quite taken in what was happening in the bed.

"So then," he began, but stopped, whirled the gun about and placed it over his shoulders, "so my suspicions were not too ill-founded . . ."

Gareth walked over closer to the bed where the two men held one another in close embrace, their lips half-opened against one another's face.

"Hey now," Gareth whispered, going very close to the men, and then kneeling down as if he were looking into a key-hole. "You never kissed me that good, did you, Sidney De Lakes . . . You never was that tender."

"You go downstairs, Gareth. Roy and I have a lot to talk about."

"No, I won't go downstairs neither. I'm going to watch this, goin' to memorize by heart what I'm seeing."

They all heard the sirens coming closer to Sturtevant's property now, then they heard the brakes and tires scream and squeal, and a man cursing. After a few minutes the searchlights moved over and into their room, catching Gareth in the eyes.

Then they heard loud profanity and outcries as the troopers discovered Brian's body.

Rushing to the window, and lifting it up fiercely so that he almost tore it from its frame, Vaisey stuck his head out into the descending night, and shouted oaths and foul language, threats and vituperation against, it almost seemed, everybody who had ever lived or breathed.

"Come on down, Gareth," a familiar state trooper's voice called up. "We have the place surrounded and we know Sidney's there with you . . . So come on down and turn yourselves in, and we can straighten this thing all out before no time . . ."

In a kind of panic, yet still cool, and holding his rifle with loving caution and poise, he turned away from the window to face the two "lovers" lying in bed.

What he observed now both sickened and thrilled him, stirred in him his deepest yearnings and passion. The two men held one another in a perfervid embrace such as angels might be capable of but which men are said to have lost. They kissed one another oblivious to any other time or place, thirstily, their longing for one another it was clear could never be appeased.

"That's right, kiss and hug all you want, go ahead, see if I care!"

Then turning to the open window, he shouted below: "We ain't never coming down till you drag us, is that clear, you shit hounds!"

A warning shot rang from below, and then Gareth, a fury aroused in him, a fury which had lain recumbent and sleep-ridden for so long, was set free, sundered from its chains, and he shot at his target below, brightly lit by searchlights, bringing the deputy to the ground.

"I got the bugger, I got him!" Gareth turned to his two friends.

But the sight of the fraternal rapt and entwined affection of Roy and Sidney made him for a moment speechless, numb, almost as mindless as when Sidney had first come to him.

"And now," he came again to the bed, squatting, bristling, "I got something to say to you two. I want you to quit what you're doin' and listen to me."

Sidney stirred and turned briefly to him to say, "Go downstairs, Gareth. March!"

"But I killed the deputy!" Gareth touched Sidney with his outstretched left hand. "Did you hear, Sid? Killed him . . ."

"I heard you, yes, but look here." He motioned to Roy whom he held in his arms.

"What about him? What about me? Are you mine, Sid . . . ? Answer me."

Gareth put down his gun and threw his arms around De Lakes.

"Tell me you're mine, Sid."

"I don't know, Gareth," Sidney replied, letting his head fall over the boy.

"What do you mean, you don't know."

A bullet from below all at once crashed through the upper part of the window pane and ricocheted off the wall, but nobody in the room paid the least attention.

"I will give you one last chance, Sid." Gareth extricated himself from Sidney's embrace. "Listen good. . . . There's a passageway through the basement where we can go. It leads to the old rendering sheds. We can hide in them if you'll go with me . . . Then we can light out together. . . . Are you listening? See, Sid . . . Quit holding him like that. Let go of him . . . You never held me like that . . . You love that filthy son of a bitch, don't you? Tell me you do, for I can see it. You love him like you never loved me. I see it, I see it!"

Gareth walked to the far corner of the room as he spoke, fingering his rifle again cautiously, barely holding it as though it were fragile or might vanish from his grasp.

"Like you never loved me," he kept repeating. "You four-flusher. Liar, murderer . . . So all this while you have lied to me about how you hated the son of the renderer and he hated you."

"I always knew he loved me, Gareth. Never said he didn't . . ." As he spoke, Sidney looked only in the direction of Roy Sturtevant, whose one hand he held in his.

"You can't love white trash like him, Sid."

Sidney's head fell over on the scissors-grinder's chest.

Another bullet, also meant probably as a warning, went through the window pane, but it struck Sidney glancingly on the arm, bringing such a gush of blood. But again neither Sidney nor Gareth nor Roy paid any mind to this. One would have thought a film was being made, and all that occurred was foreseen and practiced and therefore merely observed and tolerated, if not indeed almost ignored.

Gareth drew closer to the two men.

"Get your mouth off that carcass, Sid, and come out with me."

"I cain't, Garey . . . I couldn't even if I wanted to. I cain't run no more. I'm bushed and winded and busted from deep down. I belong with the one I have run from so long. I see that."

"Do you know what, Sid . . . ? You . . ."

A staccato of bullets hit the house now from all sides. A man's voice warned them deafeningly through a bullhorn.

"I'll give you just five seconds to tell me you love me the most, Sid, that you will leave that dirty motherfucker you're holding to your chest, and you come with me . . . Sid, you come with me, or else!"

"Else what? I'm not budgin'. I told you I have run enough . . . I won't no more."

Gareth raised his rifle.

"Then you double-crossing corpse-hunter, go join Brian and this cruddy blighter you're so stuck on . . ."

"Garey!" Sidney cried as the bullet raced through his mouth and another bullet caught him in the chest, and then oddly enough two bullets from the deputies below caught him in the head and arm, and he lay back over the form of Roy Sturtevant, who rising up then said, "What is the time now, can you tell me?"

"It's two o'clock in hell," Gareth replied and shot him twice through the head.

It took all of another day to flush Gareth out of the house. He was badly wounded and more or less incoherent, but he was still full of fight, and as the radio kept telling people who listened to it (some were listening to it then for the first time in their lives) "dangerous and armed, and protecting his own body with the bodies of his two buddies whom he had murdered in cold blood."

Neither the radio nor the police mentioned one dead man very often. That is to say, Brian McFee. They did report of course that he had been dug up from his coffin and brought to the house in what authorities believed was to have been the enactment of some weird and terrible rite. Words failed to explain it, in the phrasing of the report, and after a while the disinterred body was no longer mentioned in print or on the airways. And even at the later inquest, not much was made of it. It was whispered everywhere, though, and never forgotten in this community.

"Our little mountain town here, in remote West Virginia," Dr. Ulric had said later, "has had its veil torn away, and there have been revealed things just as terrible as those we read about in great seaports and immense metropolises the world over. Only more terrible, I do believe. . . . In my day it was the story of Jesse and Ruthanna Elder . . . Now it's these young men who have such strong passions . . . We've been brought up to date."

The sheriff himself put the handcuffs on Gareth Vaisey even as he was put down on the stretcher and borne away.

"You don't need to say anything, son," the sheriff had told Gareth that evening when he looked in on him in the hospital jail, situated only a few miles from Warrior Creek and Roy's rendering shacks and the place of the shooting. Despite the fact he was dying, surgery having been deemed out of the question, Gareth's room was heavily guarded by five or more deputies, and two state troopers, and his ward was sealed off. A television crew was waiting outside, and the story of what had happened was being reported all over the world. The mountain village Dr. Ulric had spoken of for him at such length was being called by name and discussed, photographed and documented for the eyes of five continents.

About midnight, Gareth rallied. "I want to talk about it, sheriff," Gareth began.

"The sheriff has gone home," one of the state police answered him.

Gareth took the officer's hand and held it.

"I'm not sorry for what I done," he told the deputy. "Killed them, that is."

"You can wait to say that," the man who had listened to his words commented thickly. This old deputy who had heard his words had known Gareth, as Dr. Ulric had, from birth. He had known Irene Vaisey from the time she was a girl.

"I couldn't be shut out again. I couldn't lose Sidney, you see, after I had already lost my horses, and my father and my two brothers. . . . Yet that was happening right in front of my eyes, officer! Them shutting me out with their better love-making. I was closed out . . . I had to kill them both because of the famished way they loved one another before my very eyes, you see. Like I didn't exist anymore for them, nor never had existed—they loved one another like that. That hard. It was like they was angels. They looked into one another's eyes like they had found the promised land."

The deputy called the nurse and asked her to "do something." The officer had stood up from his chair where he had listened to Gareth, but the boy pulled him down again into his seat.

"You listen to me," he said. "God damn, law or no law, you listen to me. I am making my statement and you arrogant son of a bitch, you listen to me or take off your badge and quit. . . . I had to kill them. I couldn't let Sid go over to his own enemy. Everybody knows Roy Sturtevant had been his mortal foe from the time they were both in the eighth grade, and yet here they were lookin' like they had been admitted into the gates of Paradise. . . . I warned them, but they would not listen or pay me any mind. *'You cain't go over to the other side, Sid . . . I've stood by you for a long time, and you got to remember that it was because of you and Brian McFee that I had that accident in front of the train. I would never have had that happen to me had you not initiated me into your special gang, and you know that God damn well. I am the way I am today on account of you and the renderer, for it all come through your plans. He planned to kill Brian and Brian was made to plan to kill me, all so he could have you finally to himself, and you know it. We two was just makeweights, Brian and me. He knew in the end you would fall into his lap, and you have done just that . . .'* I warned him, officer, but he wouldn't listen to reason. They were famished for one another's lips, do you hear?"

At about two o'clock in the morning the sheriff came back, and walked over to the nurse who was changing Gareth's bandages. The other officer had gone, and Gareth's eyes were closed.

"We can't give him anything more, sheriff," the nurse was saying. "He's had all the morphine now we dare administer."

"How bad does the doctor think he is hurt?" the sheriff wondered.

The nurse whispered something.

"Did you take down all I said," Gareth began after he had been silent for some minutes. There was nobody in the room as he said this, the nurse and sheriff having stepped out for a moment. His shouts and angry cursing brought the nurse back.

There were tears all the time at the rims of Gareth's eyes. The return of the nurse, and a few minutes later, the sheriff, caused the Vaisey boy to become even more voluble, and demand that all his words which contained the "truth" be taken down and given to everybody to read. He wanted to make "our simple mountain people" (as Dr. Ulric called them in moments of pique and discouragement) hear all the truth about Sidney De Lakes, the train wreck, and how Brian and he had been "betrayed."

Finally, Irene came in, but Gareth did not look at her. He never stopped talking now, lickety-split, telling how he had refused to give up Sidney to the renderer. After a moment she hurried from the room.

The next day when he was dying, Vance, accompanied by Dr. Ulric, was admitted.

Gareth started up at the sight of Vance, and put out his right hand in his direction. At that moment, Vance must have resembled Sidney more than he had at any time in his life.

Gareth motioned for him to sit down in the chair nearest the bed. Then he began at once, the same speech as before, on endlessly.

Dr. Ulric watched Vance with, if anything, more apprehension than he showed toward Gareth, who was, after all, beyond anything he might do for him.

"Sidney never kissed me the way he did Roy." Gareth's words sounded both loud and far-off to everybody assembled in the room, and Vance raised his head as if the words themselves or perhaps an explanation of them were being written on the television screen which was blank and gray before him.

But something had happened also to Vance, Dr. Ulric noted. Gareth's words, or the cataclysmic events of the past days, had relieved his ward of most of his old-maid prissiness and Presbyterian stiffness, or he had lost all that earlier when he had looked into the coffin which held his brother. *"He had no more strength in any case to keep away the truth,"* Irene Vaisey is said to have commented later with regard to him.

So now Vance listened, and nodded as Gareth spoke of forbidden kisses and embraces and hopeless love, jealousy and murder.

"They belonged to one another, Vance, and they shut me out, you see," Gareth finished.

Vance rose to go then, having, he felt, taken all the punishment he could stand, but seeing him leave Gareth cried out, calling his name over and again so that the brother of the dead man relented and seated himself once more by the bed.

"I was in love with your brother," Gareth repeated.

Vance bowed his head. Dr. Ulric fidgeted, and signaled to Vance again and again that he rise and leave.

"Where are the nurses?" Dr. Ulric began, perhaps merely to have something to say. "And where is the doctor in charge of this patient?" But in the end he too relapsed into silence, and his thoughts went back once again to the time of Jesse Ference and Ruthanna Elder, and their story which now seemed to him such a simple, naive, pathetic, and clear love idyll compared to the one that was now being concluded with the death of Gareth Vaisey, after the violent passing of Sidney and Roy.

"So you see, Vance," Gareth's voice continued, but losing its volume and eloquence, losing gradually its color and tone and emphasis, "I was deceived by Sidney and he was deceived by himself, and the only one who was not deceived was the scissors-grinder. For he knew if he waited long enough he would have Sidney, that Sidney would come to him, and that is what happened. They shut me out. So I had to shoot them. . . . And yet that only allowed them to lose me for good, didn't it, and go away after all with one another. . . ."

"I missed the funeral, didn't I?" Gareth spoke now in a voice nobody could believe was his.

Dr. Ulric had finally summoned back the nurse, but for Vance and not for Gareth, and on his instructions they brought Sidney's brother a tablet which he swallowed dutifully, indifferently, and for him contemptuously.

"Am I getting the same kind of medication Gareth has been given?" Vance surprised the doctor by inquiring.

"No," Charles Ulric replied. "Yours was something I have prescribed for you before."

"On account," Vance explained, "I would hate to tell outright, like Gareth, all the things that are on my heart and mind . . ."

Without warning, Gareth was silent. The doctor felt his pulse. But the outpouring heart Vance had spoken of still beat on, but less regularly.

Dr. Ulric asked the nurse to call in Irene again.

Irene surprised everybody then by her glacial, almost beatific calm. She had been waiting for this final summons, but she had come in without hope or expectation. Her son had never spoken to her on any of the previous occasions she had entered his sick room. She did not expect therefore to hear his voice addressed to her now.

Charles Ulric saw that she had gone beyond grief into some other chamber that is reserved for those who have lost all hope, all hint of promise or benediction, and who had found a calm, if not a peace, in the acceptance of nothing. The doctor thought her pulse must beat even more faintly than that of her son at that moment.

The rims of Gareth's eyes became redder and redder, and then the doctor realized that from the internal bleeding in his brain the red was the incessant if gradual oozing of blood, and a trail and path of blood was now beginning to course down his cheeks.

At a sign from Dr. Ulric, the nurse began wiping away the path of blood, when suddenly Irene took the cloth from her and said, "Don't . . . Please, no!"

It was then that Vance rose and gave her his chair.

The blood from Gareth's eyes ran now in little rivulets across all the features of his face, and against his lips and chin, one rivulet being joined by another, that by still another, until his entire handsome face was nothing but rivulets of blood.

It was then that Irene Vaisey lay her head down upon his face, kissing him again and again, and holding him to her more tenderly than Sidney had ever held her son, as tenderly perhaps as the renderer's son had finally returned Sidney's love and late embraces.